Donnybrook

Frank Bill has been published in *Granta*, *Playboy*, *Oxford American*, *New Haven Review*, the *New York Times* and many others. He lives and writes in Southern Indiana, and is the author of *Crimes in Southern Indiana*.

ALSO BY FRANK BILL

Crimes in Southern Indiana

Donnybrook

F R A N K   B I L L

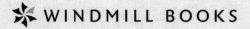
WINDMILL BOOKS

Published by Windmill Books 2014

2 4 6 8 10 9 7 5 3 1

An excerpt from *Donnybrook* originally appeared in *Indianapolis Monthly*.

Published by arrangement with Farrar, Straus and Giroux LLC, 18 West 18th Street,
New York, NY 10011, USA. All rights reserved.

First published in Great Britain in 2013 by William Heinemann

Windmill Books
The Random House Group Limited
20 Vauxhall Bridge Road, London SW1V 2SA

Addresses for companies within The Random House Group Limited can be found at:
www.randomhouse.co.uk/offices.htm

The Random House Group Limited Reg. No. 954009

www.randomhouse.co.uk

A CIP catalogue record for this book
is available from the British Library

ISBN 9780099558439

The Random House Group Limited supports the Forest Stewardship
Council® (FSC®), the leading international forest-certification organisation.
Our books carrying the FSC label are printed on FSC®-certified paper. FSC is
the only forest-certification scheme supported by the leading environmental
organisations, including Greenpeace. Our paper procurement policy
can be found at: www.randomhouse.co.uk/environment

Designed by Jonathan D. Lippincott

Printed and bound by CPI Group (UK) Ltd, Croydon, CR0 4YY

For Donnie Ross
who said it was a helluva Donnybrook,
and, as always,
for my lovely wife, Jennifer

DONNYBROOK—A scene of uproar and disorder; a heated argument.

By the eighteenth century it had become a vast assembly, held on August 26 and the following fifteen days each year, a gathering-place for horse dealers, fortune-tellers, beggars, wrestlers, dancers, fiddlers, and sellers of every kind of food and drink. It was renowned in Ireland and beyond for its rowdiness and noise, and particularly for the whiskey-fueled fighting that went on after dark. A passing reference in, of all sober works, Walter Bagehot's *The English Constitution* of 1867, gives a flavor: "The only principle recognized . . . was akin to that recommended to the traditional Irishman on his visit to Donnybrook Fair, 'Wherever you see a head, hit it.'" The usual weapon was a stick of oak or blackthorn that Irishmen often called a shillelagh. The legend was that visitors to Donnybrook Fair would rather fight than eat.

—Michael Quinion, *World Wide Words*

PART I
BURNING BRIDGES

PART I

BURNING
BRIDGES

1

I can't feed my babies, Zeek and Caleb, from jail, Jarhead Earl thought. But this was his chance to give them a better life.

He thumbed two more 12-gauge slugs into the shotgun's chamber.

The click of the first slug had echoed in Dote Conrad's ears after he'd handed the 12-gauge automatic with a full choke to Jarhead.

The barrel raised, Jarhead said, "Put your hands high. Turn to me, slow."

Dote could've grabbed any one of the rifles or shotguns that lined the wall in front of him behind the counter of his gun shop. But none were loaded.

He raised his hairy appendages. Spread them like a football field's goalposts. Hands level with his ears poking out of his brown trucker's cap, faded rebel flag across the front. He wore a gray T-shirt. Red suspenders going down over his keg belly. Brass clips pinched the waistband of his camo pants. Said, "We got layaway if you can't buy it today. Deer season's still a ways off."

Jarhead said, "I ain't buying shit. You walk to the end of the counter. I'll follow you to the safe in back. 'Less you got enough in the register."

Everyone in Hazard knew Dote only deposited his sales once a month. Kept a safe and register packed with big bills. Had never kept a loaded pistol behind the counter for personal protection. There was never a need to worry about being robbed in a small-town gun shop out in the hills of southeastern Kentucky where, after first grade, everyone knew who they'd marry and have kids with.

Dote tried, "Know times is tough. People out of work with the economy bein' in a slump. Hear the state be hiring for the road crews real soon. Whatever it is you don't have ain't gonna be got by doin' whatever it is you plan on doin' with that shotgun."

Zeek and Caleb's grit-smeared faces branded Jarhead's mind with their whining—*I's hungry, Dada*. He didn't have time for Dote's recommendations. "Let's see what you got in the register first."

"Jarhead, I can't—"

Jarhead veered the barrel two feet away from Dote. Blew a hole in the wall. The shell hit the counter. Another fell into place. Dote's ears rang as he reached for the gun barrel. Jarhead pushed into the counter. Butted the hot barrel through Dote's hands. Stabbed it into Dote's coral nose like a spear. Cartilage popped. Dote hollered, "Shit!" Tears fell from his blinking eyes.

Jarhead said, "I ain't asking."

Dote bent away from the barrel. His camo pants went dark in the crotch. Loose skin hanging from his arms wavered. Sweat creased the age spots of his forehead. He felt weak and idiotic, knowing that if he had a gun, he'd shoot this thieving bastard. He waddled to the register, cursing to himself, who'd have thought he'd bring his own goddamned ammo. Punching a few buttons, he opened it with one hand while the other pinched his nose. Pulled a wad of twenties from the tray. Then a wad of tens and fives. Laid them on the glass counter.

Jarhead ordered, "Count it so I can hear you."

When Dote counted out one thousand dollars, Jarhead shouted, "Stop!"

Half a stack of twenties remained. Dote spoke through his clogged nose. "You don't want it all?"

"Don't need it all." Held the shotgun one-handed. Reached into his back pocket. Laid a plastic Walmart sack on the counter. "Put the one thousand in the sack."

Dote stuffed the money into the sack. Blood from his busted nose dotted the bills he pushed to Jarhead, who grabbed the sack, said, "Lace your fingers behind your head. Back up. Turn around. Go into the back room."

The thought of never seeing his wife, who ate fried chicken livers breaded with her mother's secret recipe and watched the Home Shopping Network on satellite while he ran the gun shop, sent a shock of worry through Dote's body. And he pleaded, "Come on now, wait!"

Jarhead motioned the gun barrel. "Turn around!" Dote did. Walked sideways to the counter's end, where Jarhead met the rear of his head. Pressed the barrel into it. Walked Dote through the curtain into the back room, where boxes of ammunition were stacked among crates of unopened rifles. Here was the fucking ammo he needed and Jarhead told him, "Get on your knees."

Dote's face warmed with tears. Clear mucus mixed with blood.

"Please!" he begged. "Please!"

His knees cracked down onto the cold, hard concrete floor. Jarhead followed him with the still-warm barrel of the gun. Touched the rear of Dote's skull. Then Dote fell forward from the loud shudder that rippled through his body.

•

The man's flesh was charcoaled jelly. Flat dragged him from the house screaming, dropped him into the yard where he now lay with his arms spread like a deity next to a rusted tricycle. Swing set with no slide, no swings. Memories long abandoned. Smoke erupted from the flames behind them. Yellow and orange opened the night and devoured the old house.

Flat spoke. "Got to take him to an ER."

Angus cut his words. "ER will call the authorities. Two of you should've knowed better."

Liz and Angus had left Beatle and Flat to watch a batch of meth cook while they met the second shift going, the third shift coming on, at the local auto parts factory. It'd be shutting its doors in six months because of a dying economy—men and women who skipped groceries, car payments, and rent. Passed eight-hour shifts jonesing for an escape, their next dopamine rush.

The pinch-faced blisters with cooking-grease scalps,

eyes punched into skulls like recessed lights, approached Angus's goose-shit green Pinto. Passed their wrinkled wages through the rolled-down window of his car. Angus sat like a shadow while Liz took the cash, obliged the workers with a gram of marrow-clenched godliness, wiring up each buyer with the feeling of macho-supremacy.

It was how Angus had lived since the accident, and the surgery that had jumbled one side of his face into flesh puzzle pieces that no longer fit.

Angus and Liz returned to the farmhouse. Found Flat out in the yard yammering that he and Beatle had crashed hard after too many days of tweaking. Left the lithium strips pulled from batteries boiling with Coleman fuel. Before Flat could rattle Beatle awake, the fuel overheated. Off-gassed. Ignited Beatle. Next thing he knew he was pulling the poor bastard to the yard.

Now, Beatle lay digging at his oily burn and knifing their eardrums with, "Help me! Please! Help!"

Liz questioned, "So what we gonna do with him then?"

Angus ran a hand into his bibs. Removed a tool for killing.

"The shit you doing?" Flat demanded.

"Putting your mutt brother out of his misery."

Beatle's begging moistened and bounced from the soil. Angus turned the pistol to Beatle's singed hair and words found silence.

Flat stutter-stepped. Said, "Motherfuck—"

Angus raised the .45 to Flat's ash-smudged face. Pulled the trigger. Red parted white. Flat lost his shape, fell to the earth.

Liz turned away. Shook her head of chocolate-vanilla-swirled dreads. Fought tears and rattled, "Now . . . what?"

Angus slid the warm piece of protection back into his pocket. Said, "We gotta get before the county boys show up. Finger us into a long jail sentence. Go find another abandoned house to squat. Go get with your pill man. We gotta start over 'fore there's no jobs left down here, 'fore people's money runs out."

•

The shotgun blast had rattled the old man from his sleep that morning. The face on the receiving end had been unclear. The person who'd held the gun was the same one he'd been dreaming about for some time now. A sturdy male that laid miles to back road stone, jogging in the evening sun. Then he'd chiseled a beating into a stuffed military bag strung from a tree or peppered another human's build with his fists, knees, and elbows to a host of splinter-faced men sloshing booze and laying down the wagers for a winner. He was a fighter associated with the nickname Jarhead Earl.

There'd been days when he'd dreamt of sunken faces with growling bellies. Two infant boys and a female. The woman had been pained by her family. She'd thumbed a lid from a bottle. Shook pills into her palm, chewed them like Chiclets. The kids had sat in a yard of soil patched by dead grass. They played on a makeshift swing-set with a bad case of rust that had come on like acne. But when the fighter came to them, they kindled warm, as if nothing else mattered.

It was now well after dark, Purcell twisted the cap

from the bottle of Kessler, poured it into his coffee mug devoid of coffee. Placing the images that he knew were pieces of a puzzle together in his mind, just as he'd been doing for months. He lit a Marlboro, knowing there was a shit-storm forming and he'd be right in the middle of it, but he didn't know how, he was still waiting on that to take shape.

•

Flies nested and gnats hummed around the dark odor that floated from the bodies lying in the late-night humidity. Flames had taken the house's walls and roof, replaced them with a carbon structure.

Deputy Sheriff Ross Whalen stood patting a frayed blue hanky to his forehead with one hand, honing his Maglite with the other. Thinking how the town had thrived on the factory that produced profits from car and truck parts for Ford and GM but bred addiction in the laborers who found blurs in time from smoking, shooting, or snorting man-made dopamine. What would they do when the factory shut its doors? Their unemployment ran out? More jobs dried up and addictions turned violent?

Officer Meadows worked a toothpick between his cream-white teeth, shined his flashlight and watched Deputy Sheriff Whalen kneel down, and he asked his boss, "What you think, Ross?"

Glancing at the charred and the uncharred, then up at the old shack where volunteer firefighters stood guiding their own lights, taking in the black, Whalen told Meadows, "This ain't the Wild West. Houses in a small southern

Indiana town ain't s'posed to burn down like this. Nor do people end up with a bullet in the back of they brains."

Meadows spit the toothpick from his lips, down onto the John Doe's Kingsford shape, asked, "Think someone was cooking that shit again?"

Whalen exhaled. "Seeing as it's eat up most the county, I'd say so. We'll know more after the toasted Does are ID'd. The caliber of the bullet is determined. State boys and fire marshal do their investigating into how the fire started. And you get your damn toothpick up off the victim. Regardless, this ain't good."

•

Blood had dried down the back of Dote's neck. Phone line bound his hairy wrists behind his back. Cold concrete pressed against his cheek and forehead. He tried to breathe through the busted nose that had expanded into a potato turned black. Coughed. Jerked to sit Humpty-Dumpty-shaped upright, with a hammer-thumping migraine, among the stacked boxes of ammunition.

Sitting up, he found his environment was a tilt-a-whirl. Everything in the room appeared a quivered frost. The front door of the gun shop chirped behind him. Dote hollered, "Back here! Hey, help me!"

Shane rushed to the back. His right eye wandered in its socket like a fly being chased and swatted at, his left took in the worry that was Dote's outline seated on the floor. He said, "They's a mess out front. Blood and money all about the counter."

Dote told him, "Just untie me. Get the marshal over here."

Shane was the eldest of three brothers and four sisters. Traveled the back roads of Hazard by foot. He'd never owned a vehicle. Purchased a new pair of walking shoes every three months, keeping good arch support on his defined gate. He'd hair gray as the ash from the wood burnt in a Kentucky stove. Skin darker than most full-born Indians from walking in the summer sun.

"What the shit happened?"

"Been robbed and beat."

"Wondered why you's open so late. Seen the light on."

"Time is it?"

"Well past sunset."

Shane wasn't one for using numerals to tell time but understood light from dark.

"Apparently you the only one thought it odd I'd be in here after dark."

Shane flipped a Buck knife open from his front pocket. Dote heard the blade click.

"Careful with how you wield that. Don't need my wrist slit."

Shane parted the cord from Dote's wrists. Sniffed. Wrinkled his face. "What smell like piss?"

Dote pulled his hands in front of him. Rubbed his wrists. "Don't worry about it. Help me to my feet."

The front door beeped again. Dote and Shane hollered, "Back here!" at the same time.

Town Marshal Pike Johnson stepped through the curtain. "Shit Dote, come to check on you. Your wife is kindly

11

worried. Said she been calling for hours. The shit happened?"

"That fucking Jarhead Earl's what happened. Come in looking to buy a shotgun. Must've brought ammo with him from home. You know I don't keep these loaded. Robbed me of one thousand dollars."

Pike wore Rustler jeans. White T-shirt over liver-spotted skin. A straw cowboy hat atop his aging mane. A .38 snub nose pushed down the back of his waist into a clip-on holster. He'd been the marshal for twenty-some years. Had his share of break-ins. Drunks. Domestic disputes. He looked around the room, raised a lip. "Smells like some sour son of a bitch drained his vein back here."

Shane said, "Smell like piss, don't it?"

Dote got blister-faced. Said, "Probably them bottles of Fritz's Deer Lure. Spilt a few this morning."

Shane said, "Naw, this smells a bit human."

Dote huffed and spit. "Jarhead Earl robbed me, dammit! Didn't piss on me."

Shane pointed to Dote's damp crotch. "Looks like you pissed yourself, Dote."

Pike cleared his throat, asked, "You sure it was Jarhead?"

"The hell, did I stutter?"

"No need to get bitter-tongued. Just doing my job. Guess it could be expected. You all know that man his mama shacked up with wasn't his real daddy."

Shane said, "No shit?"

"No shit. His real daddy was a Vietnam vet. A marine. Was a combat engineer who did some recon, some say. Said to be a real mean sumbitch. Johnny's mama left him high and dry in Indiana, says he spoke to the dead. He never come lookin' for her either. But his mama nicknamed him Jarhead, seein' his daddy was a marine."

"Look, your job is keeping the peace. Not givin' us tall tales on that scar-knuckled meathead and deciphering the scents of human piss. How about gettin' my shotgun back along with the grand he stole?"

Pike nodded. "Kind of shotgun he steal?"

"Remington 1100. Why?"

"Looks like he left that for you. Just wanted the cash. Gun's leaned over yonder agin' the wall."

Through the curtain to the front of the store, Pike took in the situation. Money left on the counter. Specks of Dote's blood. Hole in the wall from the 12-gauge. "Don't make much sense."

Dote smarted, said, "Makes perfect sense. Boy got more pecker than he do brains. Not enough money to feed those invalid mouths he seeded with that pill-head Tammy Charles. Thought he'd steal from me."

Pike held a small spiraled notepad pulled from his rear pocket. Scribbled notes. Asked, "You say he made you count out an exact amount? Left the rest? He wanted to rob you blind, he could've made off like a goat in miles of clover. He didn't."

Dote pursed his lips. Said, "All I know is I want back what he stole. See his ass behind solid steel."

Pike closed the notepad. Slid it back into his ass pocket. Said, "I'll get an APB out. If he's home or in these hills, he'll get found."

2

Still fuming from the previous night's inferno of lost supplies and profits, Angus turned down a valley road devoid of houses for miles on either side. Cedar, oak, and birch trees lined and spread through fenced fields hot from the sun and wild with dandelions and daisies. Angus slowed to a stop when he saw a break in the fence line's wire. A farmhouse with a barn behind it sat small, almost hidden, in the distance. His arm, branded by ink, hung out the rolled-down window of the idling Pinto. A Pall Mall added hints of gray to the clear blue above. His one clouded eye met Liz's fierce stare. "What you think?"

Liz had left her '63 Oldsmobile F-85 station wagon at the Stage Stop Camp Grounds, hitched with Angus in his Pinto. Searching the curving country back roads. Passing rotted houses and beat-down trailers. Tires hanging from trees. Children hanging from mothers anchored by out-of-work fathers, who lounged in metal gliders with cans of Bud or Miller in their hands. Empties surrounding their feet like the children they disregarded.

Malice had seeded Liz's insides after what Angus had

done. Bled through her pores. Formed armies down her buttermilk complexion. She answered him, "Think if you'd have not left Beatle and Flat alone to cook that last batch, we wouldn't be looking for a third house to squat."

Angus let off the brake. Squeaked down the hill. Pulled the coffin nail to his lips, the smoke into his lungs. Braked at the mailbox. His scarred face was etched stone, letting a ghost-white exhale escape with his words. "Open that box out yonder. See if there's any mail inside."

Liz turned to the once-silver box, now the shade of waste from years of weathering. Angus flipped his coffin nail onto the cracked pavement. Liz pulled the mailbox open. Looked into the empty space. Felt her dreads knot up at the roots. Her neck popped. The side of her face thrashed the Pinto's dusted dash. She felt the heat of the day coming through the words in her ear, scented stronger than last night's house fire. Angus's eighty-grit grip released her dreads.

"Just 'cause you had a wet spot between your thighs for them two brothers don't do a thing for me. Reason we's looking for a new house to squat in is 'cause I listened to you." Angus grabbed her lower lip between forefinger and thumb. "Lose the lip 'fore I rip it off."

•

Liz rubbed the pulpy knot that had formed on the side of her face. All she wanted out of life was enough meth, cigarettes, and Budweiser to make it through each day. A stiff cock to satisfy her desire for companionship. But Angus had managed to ruin that.

Her anger kept her heated with thoughts of how or when she'd end his rituals of blame and abuse. Angus put the Pinto into park. Exited the car. Liz followed. Eyed Angus's wide back. Kept her distance.

Walking up the cement steps, he glanced up at the barn. Not confined enough for cooking crank, in his opinion—too open and spread out—but worth taking a gander at later. Looking at the white paint flaking from the wood siding of the house, Angus said, "Looks dead as Beatle and Flat, don't it?"

Liz swallowed hard. Remembered sticky nights passed with Beatle and Flat in the dark bedroom of an abandoned house. After batches were cooked and profited. Angus, gone for more supplies. Three bodies saturated with burnt chemicals. Liz crazed with endorphins. Now, the two had been left facedown. A single .45-caliber hollow-point to each skull. Men with identical last names. Connected by blood. She said, "Dead it is. Far from any eyes. No cars. No nothin'."

Angus reached for the slick metal handle of the screen door with one hand, his compact-carry .45 Para Ordnance in the other hand.

Liz asked with spite, "The hell you got that out for?"

"Just in case they's a surprise waiting in the house with a lip like yours," Angus said.

The inside smelt of must. Paths of burgundy fluid from a human paved the linoleum and cedar floors of the house as though a person or persons had been murdered. Boards creaked beneath their footing. The burgundy thickened in the bathroom. Was blotted and smeared on the sink, the claw-footed tub, the toilet seat. Curled hairs grew from a green sludge that had once been water. Angus twisted the faucet. A brown goo plopped thick then thin. Became clear as glass. He muttered, "Must have a well or a cistern."

In the dining room, Liz fingered burgundy prints that spotted a skin-tone rotary phone dangling from a curled cord. She thought about Beatle and Flat. Held the quiver of damp in her eye.

Angus pushed the .45 into his waistband. Ran a hand over the head of jet-black locks that intertwined down his spine in a braid. Eyed the water-stained ceiling and peeling walls. "Some kind of awful haunts this place."

Liz's body quaked from her hate-fueled high. She told herself this'd be a good place for Angus to meet his end after he cooked more crank. Turned to him, blank-faced. "Looks okay to me. Time to pay Eldon a visit."

•

A slanted figure stood in the barn. Metal traps in the small left hand. Rabbits stripped of fur, gutted, with their muscles stretched, were clutched in the big right hand. His one eye twitched from Bell's palsy, a paralysis that had struck him like his father had that day, the day he saw his father doing what he'd done. His face had drooped for months, after. Then slowly tightened back.

He heard the crunch of tires coming down the hole-worn drive. Peeked into the daylight, between planks of barn wood. Watched the green car pull to a stop. Door opened. A man with raven hair running down his back got out. Slammed the door shut. Then a female with hair hanging like matted red buds of dried marijuana. They walked up to the old house. The man pulled out a pistol, and they went inside.

The figure shook his head. Started to pace across the barn's hay-strewn floor. He'd lived alone, unbothered on the farm, for years. Now he'd trespassers. One with a gun. He grunted a whine. He hated guns. Wondered why these people were here, if they'd stay. He stepped to a back corner, hung the traps from a rusted spike. Pushed the straw and dust away from the wooden slats next to the table. Reached down for the iron handle. Opened the floor. Followed the stringer of steps into the hidden opening beneath the earth.

3

Eldon McClanahan was an alcoholic pharmacist who gambled his money away on horse races, ball games, and high-stakes poker. Would wager a buck on almost anything. He'd be willing to dig up and sell his mother's and father's shriveled formaldehyded corpses if it'd get him enough dough to gamble with. The man had no shame.

His wagering had won him overwhelming debt to a grain of characters running within the darker crevices of Harrison County. Word of his dilemma had reached the ears of Liz and Angus while they'd been slinging bourbon and beer at a late-night tavern. Discovered Eldon was desperate to turn coin to pay his debt and to keep on wagering. Scoped him out to use on a money project of their own devising.

A few nights later, Angus made sure Eldon met Liz in the E & R tavern over a few drinks. Eldon took her back to his ranch-style home out in the woods of Harrison County, where she threw a powerful fuck on him. Had him sitting down to piss for a week. Made him dread waking up with morning wood since Liz'd rode him raw.

After that night, Eldon would do most anything for Liz. Most especially he would happily skim tablets of Allegra-D from the pharmacy to front the ephedrine for her and Angus's meth-manufacturing scheme.

Now, having been profitable business partners for months, Liz and Angus stood on one side of the bar in Eldon's kitchen. Angus pulled on a coffin nail. Blew smoke and told Eldon, "We done got another place. Just need more them pills you been getting us."

Eldon stood on the other side. Leaned back against a stainless steel sink. Holding a glass of Knob Creek and Coke. "You still owe me for the last batch."

Angus laughed. "Done told you they ain't no last batch 'cause of the damn fire."

Eldon sipped his drink. Swallowed. Said, "Look, no money no pills. I got people I owe."

Eldon owed a certain bookie who had a collector he didn't want to meet. Had heard the stories. The collector'd pay you a visit. Paralyze your body with several needles. Do things to you. You'd pay him back in lessons of unheard-of pain.

Eldon took another drink. Liz smiled at him. His eyes fell to her faded Lynyrd Skynyrd T-shirt that held two firm breasts without a bra. Goddamn she knew how to fill a concert T-shirt. He knew how shapely those breasts were. Remembered how they'd bounced that night she rode him. Jutting up into the darkness of his bedroom when she raised. Slapping her sweaty flat stomach when her hard ass dropped onto his bony legs. Turned his white five-hundred-thread-count sheets a sweaty pink.

"Hey, two-inches-a-love, quit staring at her tits," Angus interrupted. "Say we get you three grand, you done got pills for another batch or we gonna have to wait like last time?"

Heat from the whiskey pushed Eldon's complexion to match his thin, carrot-colored hair. He stared into Angus's one blue eye, his other a gray pearl engulfed by a split-glass tint. Told him, "Look here, Terminator, you're not dealing with an amateur or you'd still be cooking cough syrup. I got enough pills right here in my backroom den for plenty more batches."

Liz ran an index finger over Angus's gray work pant leg. Stepped forward. Bent over the bar. Knowing a peek of her sugar-cookie-pale breasts would shackle the rest of Eldon's attention to her. She said, "Can I use your john? Gotta take a mean piss." She batted her thick, carved, mascaraed eyelashes in a way that seemed to say out loud, *Maybe you wanna come watch?*

Eldon tilted his mixed drink, taking in the split of pale flesh in her shirt. Imagined the sound of Liz unzipping her pants. Her powdered-donut-colored flesh meeting his toilet seat. Her warm piss splashing into the toilet. He felt the heat leave his face, travel to and harden his crotch. He tasted the smooth bourbon mixed with Coke coat his throat. Lowered the sweaty glass. Jutted his orange brows up into wrinkles on his forehead. Smiled. "Sure, sweetness, you know where it is."

He set the glass in the sink. Stepped from behind the kitchen's cherry-stained bar. His cologne-bathed body followed the side-to-side shift of Liz's ass from the kitchen's ivory tile to the hall's chocolate-stained hardwood. Felt as though he might explode wondering if she had on panties. What color they were. If they had pink elephants or blue dolphins printed on the crotch. Those were his favorites. Knowing she shaved her nether region. Then the light inside his daydream went out.

•

The man held scars. One side of his complexion had been hazed by flame. His hair raked back into a ponytail that twisted down his spine. Dye-engraved names were about his flesh like newspaper headings. He was a fighter, or had been a fighter. He was a man who'd tried to salvage what he could from life. He was hard and merciless. Then his image faded. Purcell lay in his hammock of woven rope. He'd a cigarette dangling in his right hand. Trees above offering shade. "Ballad of the Crimson Kings," a tune by Ray Wylie Hubbard, rustled in the warm breeze from a CD player on Purcell's screened-in porch. Guitar strings and banjo were being picked. Images of Jarhead ran like adrenaline in his veins. Then came the face of another man who went by Knox, Miles Knox. He and the boy Jarhead could've been twins except for age. Purcell hadn't realized until now how much they favored each other. He didn't know the man on a personal note. But he'd crossed paths with him at social gatherings where booze and talk were being passed.

Clasping his eyes, he saw a female, in her grasp was a pistol, she stared at it. In her other hand was a picture of a man she'd left, ran from—it was Knox, only younger, and he was a dead ringer for the young man that Purcell had visions of, Jarhead Earl. She lifted the pistol, tasted the metal barrel, and then the wall behind her was salted with brain and scalp. Every muscle in Purcell's body tightened, then bucked. He knew the female was Jarhead's mother.

Sitting up from the hammock, his feet smashed the grass beneath him, he reached for a sweating glass, ice rattled the liquid that was the shade of molasses. He finished the drink. Wanted the thoughts, the visions to rest. But they did not. Jarhead was traveling. It was night. There was trouble around him, Purcell could feel it. Then came the strobes of colored light and the pictures in Purcell's mind cleared. Where Jarhead was, Purcell didn't know. But he was getting closer.

•

They stood out by Ned Newton's '78 Chevy truck with a crumbling orange bed, two-tone blue-and-white front. Ned didn't want to bring the cop into his dented sheet-metal house with its damn slanted roof. Dripping AC unit hanging from a window coughing freon into what passed for the living room, where empty baggies with trace amounts of crystal lay scattered about the floor and coffee table.

Sheriff Whalen stood behind dark aviator glasses, his lips as dry as his fake words. "I's sorry having to tell you that, Ned. Know you used to run with them two. Was hoping maybe you knew who them two been running with."

Ned's pasty tongue ran over calico teeth. Wiggled them back and forth. Swollen tissue above his eyes made them appear spooned out as he met his reflection in Whalen's glassed vision.

"Nah, them two was stray of enlightenment. Was bound to happen sooner or later."

Whalen cleared his throat, knowing Ned was a lying, backstabbing piece of shit. Had yet to earn his time in a Coldcrete cell. But it was bound to happen sooner or later. "No one deserves to go out like that. Skin burnt to a crisp. With a bullet in they head."

Saturday-evening humidity pushed Ned's thinning, spider-legged hair from his buttery crown. He asked, "You talk to anyone else?"

"Poe over at Leavenworth Tavern, where they's know'd to drink. He ain't saying shit. Nor is any of the regulars. Why, you seen or spoke with them as of late?"

Ned's joints felt as though they were being chiseled. He shook his head, needing something he was out of, a bump of crank to subside this ache from within. He'd be paying Poe a visit, he thought. Told Whalen, "Been six month or better."

Whalen nodded. Knew he was being lied to. Changed the subject before he lost his temper. "Still fighting? Or you just training fighters these days?"

Ned's face lit up with a five-tooth grin. "Can't lie, Ross. I still fight from time to time to support myself."

Support your habit, Whalen thought.

Ned had been a backwoods brawler since he could place one foot in front of the other. Story was, the first time his daddy opened the backs of his thighs with a piece of leather for talking back, Ned doubled up on him. Took the belt away, punched his dad till he spit the shade of roses. Broke his jawbone. Mashed his eyes and lips. Was still hitting his father when he was pulled off him by his uncle. Who convinced his brother to take Ned twice a week to a boxing gym some thirty minutes down the river in Portland, Kentucky.

Whalen waved a hand before turning to leave, said, "You always was a mean son of a bitch. Even with this badge, I'm glad we never crossed." He thought, I'd like to cuff you. Take you out in a field of tall grass. Put one between your bug eyes. Leave you for the buzzards and opossum to chew.

Whalen opened the cruiser's squeaking door, said, "You hear anything, you know where I'm at."

•

Wet dripped from the parted cartilage of his nose. Blotted and crusted onto flared lips. Ran down his butt-crack chin. Fertilized his crop of curled chest hair. A few teeth stuck to and stained his pink Izod shirt. Eldon's tough talk had disappeared when the swelled slits of his eyes blinked back open.

His hands were twisted behind him with lamp cord, attached to the legs of the wooden chair in which he sat. A blurred outline swayed her hips in front of him. He focused. A pair of hands were pushing goose-feather-soft mounds of female flesh before him. Hank Williams blared "My Bucket's Got a Hole in It" from the radio on the kitchen counter behind her.

Angus sat next to the radio, wiping the blood from his knuckles onto a white dish towel. He'd beat Eldon pretty fair, he thought. Laid the towel down beside the three large bottles of Allegra-D. Shook his head. Said,

"Two-inches-a-love, didn't your daddy never tell you not to think with your pecker? Even with all that schooling, you're still a dumb shit." Angus pointed down at the three bottles, said, "Had to be sure you had these."

Eldon's eyes darted from Angus to Liz, who was running a hand down the front of her pants. Tonguing her lips. Giggling psychotic-like.

Eldon looked back at Angus. Slobbered, "You can't do this!"

Angus gave a Charles Manson stare. Threw both hands into the air, palms facing up, said, "Who's gonna stop me? You?" His laughter bounced into the high white plastered ceiling. Liz began to unzip her painted-on jeans. Revealing no panties, just cadaver-white flesh.

Eldon closed his eyes. Tried to fight the rush of blood. Getting hard. Shook his aching head and realized he'd no pants on. Was bare ass and balls to the wooden chair. He opened his eyes. Looked around Liz to Angus, yelled, "Untie me, dammit! We're partners!"

Angus quipped, "Two-inches, you should've been more partner-like when you had the chance, given the pills over. All you got going for you now is right in front of you."

Red drooled from the corners of Eldon's mouth. Liz's jeans slid down tight thighs pocked with slug-sized bruises. She stepped out of them. Approached Eldon. Straddled him. Pulled her worn black T-shirt over her head. Wrapped it across Eldon's face. Pressed her firm mounds up against the shirt covering Eldon's head. Behind Liz, Angus's voice said, "I'm gonna get. Let you get your two inches of fun on."

Liz smarted. "More man than you'll live to be."

Angus eyed her from behind. Clenched his fist. Swallowed his words. Not here. Not yet.

Eldon felt Liz's hand reach down into his lap. Her ass raised, she guided him into her wet. He wanted to rupture but fought it. He heard Angus's voice. "Here, take this 'fore I forget." Liz took the tool for killing.

Boots trailed away. A door opened. Closed.

Liz started to bounce with a violent rhythm. Looked at the indentations of eyes and wavering lips hidden beneath her shirt. Eldon moaned. Liz imagined the scarred face with a raven mane beneath her shirt. She couldn't forget Flat. Beatle. Or the humiliation.

Eldon felt a hard, cold poke through the T-shirt and into his temple. Liz panted, "You . . . gonna—"

Eldon panted back, "Alllmost—"

"You gonna—"

"Just about—"

"You gonna—"

"Yeah, I'm gonna—"

Eldon felt Liz lean back, intensifying the feeling. Her bare feet smacked the floor. Her weight disappeared. The poke in Eldon's temple moved to his forehead. Liz needed to know if she could do this.

Eldon whined. His legs tensed and jerked. Her finger squeezed the trigger. The jerking stopped. A mess erupted beneath her shirt.

She could do it, Liz told herself. She would do it.

4

Red and blue lights lit up the rear window of the primered Ford Galaxy. Next to Jarhead sat the Walmart sack of cash. Socks. Underwear. Cutoff jeans and a T-shirt rolled up inside also. Across the passenger's seat lay the map a fighter who went by the name Combine Elder had detailed for Jarhead. Directions to the Donnybrook in Orange County, Indiana, a five-hour drive from Hazard, Kentucky.

Jarhead'd learned about Donnybrook two nights ago, after he'd beaten Combine Elder into twelve unknown shades of purple. Afterward, Combine had smirked at the unblemished rawhide outline and wheat-tinted hair of Jarhead Earl, his razor-tight arms clawed by black and red amateur tattoos hanging by his sides. Combine told him, "Son, you oughta enter Donnybrook. You could be the next Ali Squires."

Ali Squires: Bare. Knuckle. God.

Squires was beaten only once, by a man went by Chain-saw Angus.

Combine told Jarhead that Donnybrook was a three-day bare-knuckles tournament, held once a year every August.

Run by the sadistic and rich-as-fuck Bellmont McGill on a thousand-acre plot out in the sticks. Twenty fighters entered a fence-wire ring. Fought till one man was left standing. Hordes of onlookers—men and women who used drugs and booze, wagered and grilled food—watched the fighting. Two fights Friday. Four Saturday. The six winners fought Sunday for one hundred grand.

The two jobs Jarhead worked, towing for a junkyard during the day, then flipping burgers and waffles two or three nights a week, hardly provided enough cash to feed and clothe his two smiling-eyed progeny. Boys created with the comeliest female in the Kentucky hills, Tammy Charles.

In between his jobs he jogged through the Kentucky mining hills that gave his stepfather black lung and his mother gun-powder suicide. He pounded the homemade heavy bag that hung from a tree in front of his trailer till his hands burned red. Training for his next bare-knuckle payday out in an abandoned barn or tavern parking lot. Farmers. Miners. Loggers. Drunks. Wagering on another man's will.

Altogether, the money he was making came nowhere close to one hundred grand.

Donnybrook would be Jarhead's escape from the poverty that had whittled his family down to names in the town obituaries. He just needed the thousand-dollar fighter's fee to enter.

Jarhead pulled to a stop off the side of a back road somewhere outside of Frankfort, Kentucky, worry from the robbery tensing his hands damp on the steering wheel.

"Shit! Shit! Shit! Don't need this."

The cruiser's door opened. The outline of the county

cop approached. Jarhead had his window rolled down. Watched the shadow trail toward his car in the rearview. The officer stopped at his window.

Should I open the door, punch him in his throat, his temple? Can't get caught if I'm going to help my babies and my girl, thought Jarhead.

And the officer said, "Evening. Know you got a busted taillight?"

Shit! rang through Jarhead's bones. All that worry for nothing.

Smiling, sweating, Jarhead said, "Why, no, sir. I sure didn't. Which side might it be?"

Pointing, the officer said, "Right back on your passenger's side."

"Well, I'll be having to get that fixed shortly."

"Can I see your license and registration?"

"Sure, sure."

Jarhead pulled his license from his wallet. Registration from his glove compartment. Handed them over.

Officer took them. Read over the name. Address. Said, "Long ways from home, ain't you, Johnny. Taking a trip?"

"Yeah. Going to visit friends and family up in Indiana."

"What part of Indiana?"

Nosy prick. "Down over in Orange County."

"The southern part. I got kin down in that neck of the woods myself. Who's your people? Might be some acquaintance."

This is how they catch sons a bitches, Jarhead thought. Hare-brained coincidences. He told the only name he could think, one that Combine Elder told him. "McGill. Bellmont McGill."

The officer parted a big rabbit-toothed smile, said, "Yeah, I remember old McGill. Owns damn near half of Orange County since his in-laws passed. Lots say he's rougher than a cob. Never had no cross words with him. He's tough. Not one you'd cross. Other than that, seems a fair shake. That your daddy's side or your mamma's?"

Son of a bitch must be writing an oratory on hill country families. "My daddy's."

Officer's face went odd. "Daddy's? I don't recollect McGill having brothers, nor uncles. His parents was only children, like he. How you related to—" That's when the radio on the officer's side dragged static. Came across with an all-points bulletin. "All units be advised of a black-primered Ford Galaxy. Plate number—"

Jarhead slammed his door into the officer's knees. Got out. Left-right-left-punched him to the ground while his radio spit, "Suspect Johnny Earl is considered armed and dangerous. Wanted for armed robbery in Hazard, Kentucky."

Jarhead rolled the officer facedown. Thumbed the snap open on the officer's leather cuff holder. Pulled the handcuffs out and cuffed his wrists behind his back.

Jarhead grabbed his license and registration. Stuffed them down into his pocket. Dragged the cop to his cruiser. Popped the trunk from inside the car and heaved him inside. Closed it. Drove the cruiser out into the woods away from the road. Killed the flashing lights. Tossed the keys into the front seat.

He'd made it back to his Ford Galaxy when a set of headlights came down the road. Blinded him. Stopped. A thick-bearded man sat inside an old International truck with the radio blaring—"It's All Good" by Seasick Steve. The man looked at Jarhead through the rolled-down window, asked, "Everything all right, buddy?"

Jarhead reached into his car. Grabbed his map, the Walmart sack, and said, smiling, "No, it's not. I's having some car troubles. Believe she's seen her last mile. Think I could get a lift?"

The man shook his head, said, "Why sure."

Jarhead got in. Strong waft of fuel burned his eyes. The man shifted into gear. Then offered a hand. "Tig Stanley. Don't mind the gas smell. Just doing a few nightly runs."

Jarhead shook his hand, said, "Fine by me. Name's Johnny Earl. But you can call me Jarhead."

Tig ground the gears. Asked, "Where you headed, Jarhead?"

"Orange County, Indiana."

Tig smiled. "It's your lucky night, son. I can get you to Brandenburg, where my cousin runs our business. They's a bridge'll take you over the Ohio River on 135 into Mauckport, Indiana. From there it's about forty-five minutes or better to Orange County. But I still got a few more stops to make. You give me a hand, I can pay you, get you to Orange County in a day or two."

"Fine by me long as I make it by Friday. Type of work you do this time of night out here in the boonies?"

Tig pulled a plastic puck of Kodiak from his dash. Tapped it on the steering wheel. Opened it. Pinched a chew into his lip. His eyes lit up, and he said, "You'll see."

5

Monday morning, Annus Steeprow, with her floured makeup and waxy purple lips, bounced her fingers off the McClanahan Pharmacy counter. She watched for Eldon to walk through the pharmacy's front door. Instead, a god-damned Chinaman walked in. Walked up to her.

His coal-colored hair lay neatly parted and groomed over his head. He'd serpent-cut eyes. Dry pink lips. A squash complexion. Dressed in a black dinner jacket. Silky white button-up tucked into black dress pants. He smelled of expensive cologne, spoke with an accent. "Is Mr. Eldon here?"

A few years ago, when she hit fifty, Annus had started to color her hair a crayon brown, trying to keep up with the thirty- and forty-year-olds. She was lonely. Couldn't find a man. She looked over the small man's build. He wasn't fat. Thin. Very clean. Held the hint of crisp bills. Fifties and hundreds. No ones, twenties, or fives. She'd lower a fuck on him. Be stupid not too. Told him, "Called Friday, said he's taking the weekend. He's closed on Sunday. Now it's Monday, he ain't showed up yet."

The man nodded. Reached into his jacket. His manicured hand of gold nugget rings laid a small business card on the counter. "Tell him to contact me."

Annus picked up the card. Watched the man turn around. His jacket hid his backside. Probably had no ass. She'd heard that Chinamen had flat asses. No matter, she'd still let him give her a poke or two. She wasn't an ass woman no way. She liked eyes. Dipping her tongue into them. But she didn't catch this man's eye. Watching him walk away, she spoke. "Never know about his gambling ass. Probably shacked up drunk with some trailer queen. You wanna hang around, I can call him again?"

He walked out the door. The card said, "Golden Dragon Chinese Buffet, owned and operated by Mr. Zhong." Got your number now, Mr. Shong, Annus thought as she placed the card on the cash register. Turned to the phone. Dialed Eldon, cursing him under her breath.

Eldon's father and grandfather had opened the pharmacy. Built a good family reputation in Harrison County. Left it to Eldon. Who'd also built a reputation. Probably into the Jap for plenty, Annus thought.

Eldon didn't answer. Annus slammed down the phone.

•

After calling with no answer all morning, Annus decided to pay Eldon a visit during her lunch. Drove down the paved drive. Pulled up next to Eldon's only vehicle, a rusted gray '88 Mercedes. The home was a brick ranch the shade of dead winter grass. Shingled a hunter green. Stretched to three thousand square feet. Outlined by forty-five private acres. Like the pharmacy, it had belonged to his father, was left to Eldon. Annus stepped from her Camry, fuming. "Spoiled bastard don't deserve none of this. Probably hungover again."

Robins and black birds argued in ash and oak trees while red squirrels gathered acorns from the unraked yard. Annus stepped past the two-car garage, humidity following her clicking soles down the cemented walk to the front door. Rang the bell with no answer. She pulled the glass door open. Rattled the wood with her fist. Nothing. She tried the brass doorknob. It was unlocked. Told herself that if his drunk ass had puked all over the damn house again, she'd be damned if she'd clean it up. Even if he rode the wrinkles out of her ass again using the secret portal.

Opening the living room door, she smelt an odor reminiscent of spoiled cabbage combined with pork past its expiration. The wave of rot throughout made Annus's powdery complexion wrinkle with sweat. She waved her hand back and forth in front of her face, shaking her head. Entered the kitchen. Then screamed. And screamed. And screamed.

•

Annus dialed 911 in between bouts of vomiting hysteria. Gave her statement to Officer Meadows when he arrived. Told of Eldon phoning Friday. Taking the weekend, not showing up this morning. Or answering his phone. Also, a Mr. Zhong had stopped in looking for Eldon. So she came to check on him during her lunch.

Deputy Sheriff Whalen pushed his hanky over his mouth, blocking the sour waft of Eldon's details. Hands behind his back. Attached to an oak chair. No pants. A mess of piss and fecal had leaked from the chair to the tile floor. Forehead opened in its center with eyes holding a dead stare. Brain matter and skull flung about the rear of his head like pasta garnished with chunks of tomato. A few teeth knocked from his mouth, stickered to his pink shirt. A single .45 brass casing on the floor.

Meadows stood beside Whalen, asked, "What you make of this?"

"If State Police forensics match fingerprints and ballistics from that brass on the floor to the other two murders, I'd say Harrison County has got more than a meth problem, it's got a world of shit."

6

Ned believed in two relaxed hands forming fists, a bump of crank in each nostril, before he threw that first punch. When he learned from Deputy Sheriff Whalen that Flat and Beatle had been running crank without his knowing, he became far more interested in finding the source for personal joy rather than catching his friends' killers. He'd burnt every bridge he had with crank cooks and dealers in every surrounding county for a hundred miles.

Daylight peeled the dark away when the Leavenworth Tavern's door swung open, ringing the bell above the entrance. Letting everyone know another of them had arrived to burrow his head down into the foam-topped glasses of gold that made the realities of everyday life bearable.

Ned seated himself on a round vinyl stool, called for a Natural Light. Poe slid the silver cooler open, pulled out and popped the can, set it in front of Ned. "Sorry to hear about your buddies."

Ned evil-eyed Poe, yearning for something more than the ice-cold can. "Old habits die hard."

Poe nodded and asked Ned, "Guess you'll be leaving

soon, going down to the 'Brook this year?" Poe was a contact for the Donnybrook, someone who directed fighters and onlookers to its whereabouts, had a quota to keep McGill happy.

Ned sipped his beer, swallowed, and said, "Yeah, that's why I come here. I need a little edge. I know you know who Flat and Beatle's running with, know they's pushing some crank for a cook."

Poe wiped the bar with his towel, glanced down the booze-stained surface feeling as though he'd just ate a handful of molasses-coated thumbtacks. Poe didn't want in the middle of this. "I don't know nothing."

Ned was already halfway up across the bar. "You can lie to Deputy Sheriff Whalen, but you lie to me, I beat your mouth into a permanent grin."

Poe was no fighter. But he knew Ned's nine lives of beating and robbing crank dealers for their money and product had about give out. Telling him wasn't doing him no favors. Poe spread his old cordite-muscled arms across the bar, rested on his palms, said, "Look, they met a piece of tail in here months back. Started running with this gal and some other guy. Big bastard with ink all up and down both arms. Hair dark as charred wood. He'd an accident with a chainsaw. Got one eye all whited over with bite scars. Said he used to own a logging company till the economy went to shit. Started cooking crank to turn coin."

Ned had stopped listening when he heard the word *tail*. When Ned wasn't using his fists or inhaling crank, he was buried asshole deep in snatch. Sloppy-joe big or tweak-starved thin, he liked them all. His pupils expanded with excitement. He asked, "What the tail look like?"

Poe ran a hand over his peeled head, crinkled one eye small, leaving the other large, said, "She'd the shape of a death angel. Girl'd fuck you with her eyes not even meaning to. Just a whiff of her swagger make you feel like your balls was blued. She'd a fucked-up wad of hair like that Bob Marley. But her figure was pure poison. The guy never come in much. But she, Flat, and Beatle used to all the time. Sold crank to some of the regulars. But since the deaths, ain't seen sight of either them."

Ned asked, "They crank any worth?"

Poe's teeth shone like lemon-colored ammonia. His eyes glittered bright too. "It's prime."

Ned asked, "Don't know where else they'd hang, do you?"

Poe was short with, "Nope."

Ned was running a thought through his dirty double-crossing mind, said, "I got a few days 'fore I leave for the 'Brook. Here's how this is gonna work. I come in here open to close"—Ned pointed to the back corner by the jukebox—"and sit back yonder. You point them out to me if they come in."

Poe exhaled, lowered his head, pretended to think it over, telling himself Ned's day of chastisement could be around the corner, he was just hastening him along. Raised his head, muttered, "Sure, Ned, sure."

•

It took a week to replace what Angus had lost. He bought rolls of duct tape, cans of spray paint, and boxes of garbage bags to black out the house's windows. Attached the garbage

43

bags with the duct tape, spray-painted any crack of light to keep stray eyes from nosing. Placed a hotplate burner and a Coleman camping stove to the west of the house's kitchen, next to a box-fanned window, where they'd litter night and day with combustible gases.

A generator sat outside with containers of unleaded. Extension cords delivered 500 watts to each aluminum clamp light in the house, 1300 watts to each of the tripod lights, creating a brightness to the dark work at hand.

The rest of Angus and Liz's supplies came from untraceable sources. Boxes of mason jars. Gallon jugs of distilled water. Bottles and containers of Liquid Heat, Liquid Fire. Packages of batteries. Ammonia. Canisters of Coleman fuel. Coffee filters. Rubber bands. Empty pop two-liters. Rock salt, latex gloves, clear tubing, and a fire extinguisher.

Angus soaked a bottle and a half of Allegra-D in a Pyrex bowl of distilled water. Separated the junk to the bottom, rendered the ephedrine into a separate dish. Added a bottle of Liquid Heat. Placed the combination onto the Coleman stove, began cooking the mix into a toxic paste. Liz stood outside the kitchen window, her eyelids batting like moth wings around a white light. The low-level hum of the box fan pulled fumes from the kitchen, blew them into her face.

She tilted her head back. Nostrils flared on the inhale, she said, "Dammit, that shit'll get you going."

Latex gloves covered the pit-bull tattoos that gnawed through the tops of Angus's hands. He scraped the cooked matrix from the bowl, emptied it into a large mason jar. Cut the tops off batteries. Pulled out the lithium strips, careful not to overdo it. Too much lithium in the product added cramps to the user's joints. Once word got out about a cook's crank giving the aches, they'd lose their gain. He measured and added the ammonia. Placed the jar onto the hot plate till it began to bubble like an underground eruption on the ocean's floor. He controlled the heat. Kept the bubbles from subsiding but also from boiling over and exploding. Waited for the bubbles to stop, lowered the heat, let the jar sit, watched the good settle to the bottom.

Empty smaller jars lined the weathered wood table in the kitchen. A heat-resistant rubber band secured a coffee filter to the opening of each. Angus poured the large mason jar of cooked material into them. Separated the good into the jars, the filters keeping the bad. He filled each mason half full. Removed the coffee filters. Took an empty plastic two-liter, placed a funnel into its opening, poured in a bottle of Liquid Fire. Removed the funnel. Filled the two-liter a quarter full of rock salt. He watched the concoction smoke, twisted the two-liter's lid back on with a clear tube inserted through it and secured by duct tape. Held the two-liter above each of his small masons, pushed the clear tube into each opening, smoking the contents into a wet snowy powder. Then he strained the contents of the small masons through coffee filters for the last time.

Angus took a few sample bumps chased with two kettles of thick coffee for the second and final batch. Repeated the process. After ninety-six hours, he'd a mess of corrosive white powder that he bagged into Ziplocs. Over six hundred doses. Bringing Liz and him more than a hundred and twenty dollars per dose.

•

Lurking like a feral ape, the configuration studied the tin-framed screens of the farmhouse's kitchen windows, sniffed the fried heat that came toxic and caused his eyes to bat and bulge. What he could make out through each opening was sheened and slick, almost rubbery, but he could get no glimpse. Stepping backward, he poked at the thin fibers with the corroded curve of a corn sickle he carried, watched it indent. He twisted his glance and saw that each window was covered by a black film or drape. And for the first time in months he cursed, lisped words fell in a slobbering start and stop, saying, "Sh . . . sh . . . shit!" Though it rolled from his tongue like, "Ch . . . ch . . . chit!" A muffled sneeze.

Stepping to the other side of the house, he ducked down when he noticed the windows were not covered, could smell the hints of cigarette smoke, peeked in from the corner. Saw the embered tobacco burning bright then dim. A slab of man sat shirtless, his back pressed into the crumbling paste and paper of a wall. With his head leaned back, every time he puffed on the cigarette it'd light up his face and torso with the shadowing of letters about his frame and a pearl glob for one eye sprayed by disfigured skin.

On the floor lay a female curled on her side, the slow rise and drop of her ribs. The figure felt his pulse redline with sadness as he watched her sleep, just as he'd done his sister, who'd been seeded by a neighbor boy. The shape of her stomach growing rounder and rounder over the weeks. Before his daddy came from the woods, delivered the horror that screamed like an engine laying tire skids on a road of carnage. He wondered how much longer these two lopers would squat. Felt as if his privacy were being invaded. He watched the man stub out the smoke, reach for a mound to lay beneath his head. Without the cigarette's glow the room was blanketed by dark and the figure stood with these memories haunting him as he backed away from the house, started for the woods to check his animal traps.

•

They slept like two fetuses in a womb. Warmed by sleeping bags and lantern light.

Twelve hours later, they ate food they'd packed in coolers of ice. Bologna or ham blanketed by cheese, mashed between slices of bread. Garnished with mustard. Washed down with bottled water. Sides were bags of chips. Desserts were unfiltered Pall Malls. Trash was packed in large Hefty bags, later dumped in nearby hollers or in the Leavenworth Tavern's dumpster. They lived like gypsies during an apocalypse. Had been surviving in this way going on a year.

Smoke whispered into the air from Angus's Pall Mall dangling from his lip. He dragged a metal feeding trough from up by the corncrib that sat off from the barn. Dragged it through the high weeds down to the house, next to the old apple tree, where Liz stood shaking her knotted buds of hair, asked, "The shit you fixing to do with that?"

His lungs felt as though someone'd dropped an old Pontiac's rear end down on them, and he heaved, "Figure we'd need a good cleaning before we go out. Do our rounds tomorrow night. Need to wash the chemical stink from our asses. You might need double what with the chemical and dead fuck stench from Eldon."

Liz pushed the corner of her lip up into a smirk, wondering how she'd make him meet his end, said, "Ain't got no hot water."

Angus pointed to buckets stacked next to the house. "You can fill them metal buckets with water, heat them on the hotplate and the Coleman."

Liz said, "Think I'm gonna step out in all these weeds? Get ticks and chiggers biting all up in my privates?"

Angus finished his coffin nail. Wiped the beaded stink from his wool brow, said, "I'll see what I can cipher up at the barn, clean out this area of weeds. Take yourself inside, start heating them buckets."

Opening the barn door, Angus felt eyes shadow his every creaking step across the wood floor coated with straw. Overhead, rafters ran gray with dust and thick puffs of webbing. A roll of twine hung from a far wall. In the right corner sat a metal table sandblasted by age. Two chairs with busted vinyl cushions pushed beneath. He walked to it, fingered the pages of a Sears catalog from the early eighties. A checkerboard sat beside it, each devoid of dust.

Along the right wall hung a ditching shovel, pick, double-sided axe, maul, barley fork, pitchfork, sickle, potato planter, bill hook, and root pick. All looked crafted by hand. Antiques from a time long forgotten. On down the wall, various-sized hunting traps decorated the barn wood. Smooth metal mouths closed, rouged by blood from the captured.

Angus fingered the handle of his .45, his eyes taking in

silence's movement. He smelled a hint of lye. Felt as though eyes were following his hand grabbing the sickle. But he knew not where the eyes were or if it was just paranoia from all of the crank cooking.

•

Rocking in a rusted metal chair, Angus sat in the uneven lengths of yard, scented of soap, watching the night for any hint of trespass.

The screen door squeaked open, slammed into the frame from behind. Liz pressed an ivory hand onto his cotton-shirted shoulder, glanced down at the .45 in his lap. "The shit you doing?"

"Can smell wood smoke."

"So?"

"So it's summer. What the shit someone need a fire for?"

"Don't know, maybe cooking? Who cares. I'm going over to the tavern, get some smokes. Toss a few drinks. You wanna saddle up, ride shotgun?"

"Watch you get glass-eyed for stray cock? I'll pass."

"Suit your damn self."

Liz turned. Angus yelled, "Hey, get me some smokes while you're cock hunting—Pall Mall."

You're good as buried, Liz thought. Said, "Sure." Walked down to her station wagon.

Angus gripped the Para Ordnance handgun in his lap, looked out into the barnyard of weeds, listened to Liz's wagon fire up as he told himself, If someone else is squatting around this place, they gonna get opened up wide and buried deep.

•

The figure sat in the soggy darkness turning the spit every so often to brown the muscled creature, careful not to burn any angle of its pink. The spit was set end to end into the makeshift stove of limestone rock piled into a boxed pit. He kept the fire at night with chunks of cedar and tangy spruce, making orange coals to simmer in the daylight, keeping the smoke unseen, not wanting any attention from the outside world.

Several nights ago he had smelt the strange burning rotating from the farmhouse's kitchen window, wondered what they were cooking and went to investigate before he disappeared into the woods, guided by moonlight and stars to check his traps. Animals flailing with metal teeth biting into their hinds till he pressed a boot into their necks, wielded a blade down across their throats.

He had stored the meat in a large wooden barrel he'd sunk into the earth next to his water source at the bottom of the darkness in which he sat. Insulated the outside of the barrel with stone and silt, built a wooden box, sealed the cracks with red clay, placed it over the barrel's opening to maintain a cold inside the barrel. It was something he'd learned from his father.

Potatoes and carrots from his hidden garden were pushed down into the coals. Removed them with a tin shovel. He'd lived here off the land in this way since that day years ago, knowing only the farm, the land he trapped and hunted within the valley.

He'd watched the towering man enter the barn. Same man he'd watched smoking nights back. Sized him up as he gazed at the tools and animal traps on the wall. Watched one of his long arms decorated with inked lettering, vines, and skulls remove the sickle from the wall while his other arm touched a gun handle pressed down the front of his waistband. The sight drove a shiver through the figure.

He pulled the spit from the flame with an animal-hide glove, blowing on the meat to cool it, wondering what the man and woman were doing in the old house, what they were cooking the other night that smelt so god-awful. Biting into the meat, he hoped they'd leave soon. Or he'd have to bring chaos to the farm like his father had years ago.

7

Liz's ass swung from side to side. The sound of John Prine's voice amped from the jukebox: "But Your Flag Decal Won't Get You into Heaven Anymore." Every gap-toothed male's bloodshot eyes branded holes through the denim on her left and right ass cheeks. Especially the man sitting alone in a dark corner of the Leavenworth Tavern.

Smoke and booze warmed her body. Made her feel at home as she pressed herself onto a worn barstool. Pulled a wad of bills from her front pocket and met Poe's surprised eyes. "Ain't seen you here in a few. What can I get you?" he said.

Liz smiled without trying, feeling all the eyes on her, happy to have distance from Angus. Glad he didn't saddle up shotgun. Running her tongue over thick lips, she told Poe, "Five packs of Pall Malls, two shots of Turkey 101, bottle of Bud, and two dollars in change."

Poe winked. "Making up for lost time, I see."

Turning his back to Liz, he grabbed the smokes, opened the cooler, removed the cap from a bottle of Bud. Set those in front of her. Turned back to the bottles of whiskey that lined the mirror behind the bar. On his way back around, made eye contact with a far corner beyond the bar. Nodded his prickled head. Poured two shot glasses of Turkey, set them in front of Liz with her Bud already half gone. He told her, "That'll be thirty-five even."

Liz pulled two twenties from her wad of bills and said, "Don't forget my two dollars in change."

Two shots back to back ignited Liz's tonsils. She chased the burn with her beer. Told Poe, "Get me another Bud." He obliged. She took her loose change and fresh beer, stepped past the sex-starved stares of working-class and full-time drunks, made her way to the jukebox. She entered two dollars' worth of quarters, flipped through the selections, punched in some Skynyrd. "The Ballad of Curtis Loew" and "Call Me the Breeze."

She sat back down at the bar. Finished her Bud. Ordered another. Laid a twenty out, said, "Keep 'em coming." Poe nodded, set her down another beer.

She fingered the cold bottle, knowing that after what she had done to Eldon she could kill Angus. But she had to be smart about it. He was clever. Not a man to cross. But she wanted him to suffer. Not by torture. Just a slow death. Like slitting his wrists, ankles, and throat. Leave him to bleed out in battery acid. That was an Old Testament idea.

She could shoot him, but she'd need a gun. Could maybe get one of his pistols. Only he kept those close and hidden. She took a swig of the Bud, telling herself she was already tired of thinking about it. Needed a good buzz. A stiff dick. Something to whittle the edge off.

Beside her a man's voice growled, "Poe, get this fine piece of ass another Bud and shot of Turkey. It'll be on me."

Liz turned her attention to her new benefactor. He'd been kicked around by the years. His hair thinned back over his ears like threads of twine. His brows were swelled and spongy, eyes bored into his head. Cheekbones pulled tight with scars, worked down into a clean shave. The wired muscles of his body sat hidden beneath a navy blue Lucas Oil T-shirt tucked into Dickie jeans and work boots.

Liz said, "Thank you, Mister—"

The knuckles of his hand were flat like Angus's, not round. His long fingers swelled around a can of Natural Light. He took a sip, said, "Ned. Just call me Ned, sugar."

"Well, Ned, what brings you here?"

Beneath the dim bar lighting his lips parted. He'd a mouth of staggered teeth. Missing more than his gums held. Taking in Liz's shape, he thought he'd never seen something with such vile beauty. He could see the poison Poe'd spoke of. Felt it in his loins same as the yearning for a bump, and he said, "Looking for some crank."

Keeping her eyes on the man, Liz swigged her Bud. Acted surprised, said, "Crank?"

He pushed his forefinger to his right nostril, inhaled hard. "Crank, godliness, crystal, whatever you wanna call it."

She laughed, ran a fingernail up into the hem of his shirt sleeve, said, "You old bone. Now, what would a sweet girl like myself know about something illegal like that?"

Ned flashed a meth-mouth smile, wanting to embed his old bone in her, said, "Sugar, just letting you walk God's earth is illegal. Word around this here tavern is that a female shaped like hunger peddles some high-grade shit from time to time. Maybe you ain't that female. Either way, the drinks is on me and it was nice making your acquaintance, Miz—"

She grasped his arm. Dug her nails into his biceps. Said, "Call me Liz. Say I am that shape of hunger. How much you craving?"

"However much you got."

Liz released his arm, asked, "How I know you good for it?"

Ned dug down into his pocket. "The Ballad of Curtis Loew" ended. He laid down a thick coil of bills. "Call Me the Breeze" started. Ned tongued his broken teeth, said, "I'm good for it."

Liz smiled sucrose-sweet. Her eyes went Asian-thin. A gunshot went off in her mind's eye. The plan hit her all at once. She said, "Ned, I got a deal for you."

•

From the pitted cast-iron skillet on the gas stove came the pop and sizzle of green tomatoes that'd been soaked in buttermilk and breaded in cornmeal and cracker crumbs. Purcell stood over the rust-colored counter, pressing the steel of a skinner against a gray rectangular stone that'd been lubed by 3-in-1 oil. He was honing an edge. Thinking about what he'd read in the newspaper earlier in the day, about wage cuts and unemployment. How companies across the U.S. were in a slump. Some were sinking while others tried to do more with less. The American way had expired, been lost somewhere. Now it seemed to work in the U.S. just meant you were a number trying to make big numbers for the men above you. And if you couldn't do it, there was another number that could.

Forking the crumb-coated slices, Purcell turned each piece in the grease as the sounds of a barking dog arced through his mind. The shouts of a female came, and faces, inflamed and hurting. Jarhead was in a vehicle. Beside him was a man who went by the name Tig. And Purcell knew that batch of bad the man was associated with. He'd ties to a man named Dillard Alcorn. Gunrunner. But Tig took his shut-eye across the river at Alonzo's place, and they dealt in all manner of crime and young skin to turn coin. And like always the visions stopped. Purcell knew he'd need to start packing, as it was only a matter of time before the arrival.

•

When Jarhead saw a light come on inside the house, he cursed under his breath. He stood out in the country road by Tig's truck with the cloak of night all around, the truck running with the lights off. This was the fifth and final house.

A full moon guided Jarhead's quick jaunt up the drive. He watched each room of the house come to life with light, the shadow inside bouncing from room to room. Jarhead's heart raced, him hoping he'd make it to Tig before the shadow did.

Out back of the house a dog barked. Sounded like it weighed two hundred pounds.

Tig lay under the rear of the truck. Gas container. Small

hose. Handheld, battery-powered drill. Maglite. Gas being siphoned from the tank and into the red container. Tig and his cousin would sell it for a cheaper price than was paid at the pump.

The creak of the door went unheard. Light footsteps across the wooden deck. Down the steps. Into the dew-covered grass. A single-barrel 20-gauge lifted the same time Tig stood up. He heard the click and then the voice. "You thieving piece of—"

From behind, Jarhead wrapped a sleeper choke on the man with the shotgun. But not quick enough. An explosion lit up the dark, hollowed everyone's eardrums. Lead dinged against the truck. Shattered the driver's side window.

The barking dog went psychotic behind the house, whining and howling.

The man dropped the gun. Tried to stomp Jarhead's boot with a bare foot. Reached for the arms around his neck. Scratched and dug into Jarhead's forearms. Jarhead held tight. The fight slowed. The man went limp. Jarhead let him fall to the ground. Stepped across the yard over to the truck. Found Tig pushed up against the back tire. Moonlight beat down on his shaking body. "Goddamn that was a rush," Tig huffed.

Dark moisture ran from Tig's leg. Jarhead sucked air, said, "Looks like you got hit."

"Can't feel shit," Tig grunted, offering a hand to Jarhead. "Pull me up. Let's push some back road 'fore the shit gets too deep for wading."

Behind Jarhead, the house door opened. A woman's voice screamed back into the house, "Sarah! Sarah! Dial the county police. They's men out here done shot your daddy! They stealing his truck!"

"Fuck!" Jarhead shouted. "Fuck!" Took Tig's hand and pulled him to his feet. Reached for the gas containers. Tig said, "Give me one them sons a bitches, boy." Jarhead helped Tig across the yard, each weighted down with a container in tow, half running toward the road where the truck sat idling. Tig laughed. "Ain't this fun?"

The lady barefooted across the deck. Down into the yard. Found her husband while her daughter rang the police. "No!" the lady screamed. Started off behind the house. Kneeled down at the maniac dog. Said, "Grim, calm your ass down." Unlatched the heavy chain. Said, "Now these sons a bitches gonna get theirs."

At the truck, Tig slung the gas into the rear. Out of breath, he told Jarhead, "You gotta drive. My leg is fucking burgered."

Jarhead said, "All right." Opened the passenger's side door. Heard steps pushing through the damp yard. Then a low growl followed by the lightning-fast roar.

Tig hollered, "Fuck!" Fell against the truck's bed. Tried to kick. Punched and pushed at the black German shepherd that came up on its hinds. Laid its fronts on his chest, its mouth gnawing into his right arm.

"Get this bastard off me!" He shrieked like a teething child.

With no gun, knife, or makeshift billy club, Jarhead did the only thing he knew to do. Balled his fist and punched the mauling shepherd in its head. Once. Twice. Then its ribs. Grim yelped, fell, and ran.

Tig lay against the truck, breathing heavily. Moisture running now from his leg and arm, smearing the side of the truck. He panted, "You about a mean son of a buck. Gonna have to buy you a few rounds."

Jarhead helped Tig into the passenger's side. Told him, "Don't owe me shit." Slammed the truck's door. Heard the sirens coming from afar. "Shit!" Got in on the driver's side.

Asked Tig, "The hell you want me to go?"

Fuel rimmed Tig's hands and clothing, combined with the red that seeped from his peppered wounds. He laughed. "Get me to my cousin's. He take care of me. Pay you good."

"Just give me some damn directions. Got no idea where I's at."

Tig said, "Keep going down this road heading west till you see the signs for Brandenburg. Follow them."

Jarhead stomped the gas just as the road behind him lit up.

•

Liz stumbled through the kitchen door. Three lanterns glowed from the counter, shadowed the packs of smokes she threw onto the table littered with jars, bottles of Heat, coffee filters, rock salt, and Ziplocs. She grabbed a lantern, went into the dining room, picked up the two ten-gallon buckets that held the baggies of meth. Took them into the kitchen. Sat down in a chair, broke the lid open on one of the buckets, pulled out one of the baggies. Fingernailed a snort into her nose. Felt the jolt kick the booze buzz in the ass, pushed the baggie into her pants. Sealed the bucket and waited.

From the back bedroom through the dining room his voice was a fist in the mouth. "The shit you doing?"

He'd become too predictable. Her eyes were two faded stars looking at him. She said, "Got us a buyer. Wants it all."

"Buyer?"

"Name's Ned." She smiled.

Lantern light bounced shadows over the uneven meat of his eye, highlighted Angus's disgust. "Who vouched for him?"

"I did. Showed me a fat wad of dough."

Angus's words sparked with anger. "Showed you his fat prick, probably. Don't know that many around this county. Could be he's a narc. We deal with people that've been vouched for."

Liz played dumb, said, "We deal at the factories."

Angus could ignore Liz's poor choices in the sack but not to whom they sold meth. He didn't flinch. Gave her a quick palm to the mouth. Knocked her backward in the chair. Her head rattled against the floor. Angus said, "You wanna be a stubborn bitch hound, I treat you like one." He spat on her. Stepped back. Pulled a smoke from his T-shirt pocket, a lighter from the table, fired up a glow. Said, "I make the deals. Done let you and them two brothers front that shit at the tavern. Now they's dead."

Liz pressed two hands onto the floor, pushed herself up. Blood rivered from her lip. She laughed. "Ned's gonna get it and you gonna get what you gave, fucker."

When the screen door cracked open, Angus squinted,

noticed the barrel too late. Felt the fire that filled his ears with combustion, his inhale with burnt gunpowder. He hit the kitchen counter, dropped to the floor quivering, eyes rolled into mothball whites.

Liz stood up. "Bastard!"

Ned pushed into the kitchen. Stepped over, nudged Angus's leg with his boot, leveled the barrel between his eyes. Liz pushed the barrel away. "Let his ass suffer, let him bleed out. Looks like you about got his heart anyway."

Ned asked, "Got the shit?"

"Right there." Untrusting, Liz grabbed the buckets of meth. Said, "Let me get somethin'." Walked through the dark house to the back bedroom. Set the buckets down. Rummaged through the moonlit room. Picked up some of her clothing, pushed it into her rucksack. Saw the outline of Angus's pistol on his sleeping bag. Pushed it in with her clothing, along with a box of shells. Zipped up the pack. Slung it over her shoulder. Grabbed the buckets. Walked back into the kitchen. Asked Ned, "Where to?"

Ned held the shotgun in one hand, reached his other down onto Liz's ass, squeezed, and said, "My place, get the rest of this deal going."

8

Touching the screen door's handle, the slanted figure inhaled sharply. The musty burn from inside the house couldn't cloak the memory of what had taken place years ago. He pulled the door open with his big hand while his smaller hand, missing halves of the last two digits, wrapped around a long-edged piece of steel.

From the barn, he'd heard the blast. Remembered hearing several of them that day his family was murdered. But tonight he'd watched two outlines walk from the house after the gunshot. Listened to the rumble of their separate engines. Lights, one after the other, drove down the road. Turned out into the valley and disappeared.

Inside the kitchen, lantern light revealed a table of scattered objects. Car keys. Packs of cigarettes. Coffee filters. Mason jars and shapes the figure didn't recognize. On the floor below the sink, his head propped against the metal cabinets, lay an array of carnage. The man he'd seen arrive with the woman a week ago, now reamed about the left side of his chest.

The man lay in the exact spot he remembered his father

standing when he'd startled him that day long ago, coming in from the woods after hunting squirrel. Creak of the screen door. His father's face twisted to meet his own. Red beaten with damp. Short of breath. Hair in disarray. Talking in a string of unfamiliar syllables. Then he'd followed the female screams that bounced from the bathroom. Where he discovered his mother, Azell, his sisters—Doddy, who was pregnant, and Tate, slow-minded but beautiful—each bound by twine. Approaching them, he'd felt his father's hands clamp around his neck from behind.

He shook the memory turned to blemish from his thoughts. Stepped down on the man's chest. Didn't see a gun tucked anywhere on the man's frame. Pressed the piece of steel into his neck. Wanted to see if he'd any fight in him or if it was freckled about the floor and cabinets.

He bore down into the man's face. One side smooth. The other gnawed. Uneven. His eyes followed the wet scattered about the man's neck and shirt. It ran from the left shoulder, an explosion of skin, vein, muscle, and bone.

The figure felt the rise and fall of the man's chest beneath his boot. Turned his attention to the tic of the man's left hand.

Angus shuddered through the pain. The voices gone. His mouth tasted of desiccated soil and slug shot. The name Ned hammered heavy in his mind like the weight on his chest, the festering ache in his left shoulder.

What the fuck! Angus made out the towering shape pressed down on his chest with unmanaged husks of hair, one arm of length grasping a machete, the other hanging small, malproportioned from its socket. The shape appeared muscled like the bare roots of an oak tree. Wore a crimped white dress. It was staring at Angus's left hand.

Angus's nerve endings tensed, his heartbeat thrusting as though he'd had a few bumps of crank. The shadow turned back to him. In one motion, Angus bit through the pain. His right hand grabbed the shadow's left leg. Shifted his left hip with his own left leg. Knocked the shadow to his right. Got from beneath the shadow's weight.

The figure fell into the counter. Lantern light in his eyes. Unfazed, he turned around blinking. Watched Angus push his back against the wall, using it to stand up. Appeared all of the man's fight wasn't shed about the floor and cabinets, least not yet.

The rush of blood loss and tic of pain wobbled Angus. Taking in the shadow, he gasped through clinched teeth, "The hell are you?"

The shadow stuttered, "Gr-gr-gravel."

Taking in the machete that Gravel held, Angus feared its use on him and rushed the beast, shouldered and clutched the shadow. Squeezed and inhaled the scent of a musty rodent bathed in lye. Cut off any chance of a swing or swipe of the machete. Suffocated his one arm. Gravel elbowed his free arm into Angus's shoulder. Pain chipped Angus's insides.

Angus looked into the shadow's face, two angered eyes beneath dead strands of hair. The shadow grunted. "St-st-stop." Angus ignored his word. Reared his head back. Drove his forehead forward repeatedly. Cartilage separated from red. Lips blued.

The shadow wailed. Let go of Angus. The machete

clanged to the linoleum. The ache of Angus's shoulder dropped him to his knees. He twisted his body. Felt the burn of a rubber-soled boot indenting the side of his face. Then the knot of bone flailing his temple, causing his eyes to dart and his vision to blur, when a hand crimped his wound, his mind went south from the pain and his thoughts ceased.

The shadow who called himself Gravel sat winded, looked upon this man who lay in a home that had been unoccupied for years because of the onslaught that had taken the innocent, innocent that had once been his family. He watched the ooze expand from the man's busted ball of fiber and thought enough blood had been spilt for tonight. He would mend the wounded man.

PART II

REAPING THE FLAMES

9

Deputy Sheriff Whalen handed the sheet of paper to Detective Thurman. "The shit's this?"

Whalen replied, "APB on Johnny Earl from a few days back. He robbed a gun shop way down in Hazard, Kentucky. Beat a county cop on a back road outside of Frankfort, Kentucky. Ditched him and his car in the woods. Ain't been seen since. Could be coming our way."

Thurman asked, "How's the cop?"

Whalen said, "He's breathing. Gave a full description. Johnny Earl said he was on his way to visit kin in Orange County. It didn't check out. Just passing it along. So what you got on Eldon?"

Detective Thurman told Whalen, "Toxicology from Eldon's body matched the contents of the glass in his kitchen sink."

Whalen sat behind his desk and asked, "So he was drinking and—"

"And maybe had a disagreement."

The two men looked to be in their late forties. But Thurman—unlike Whalen, who was light-heavyweight hard—was power-lifter big. Each had grown up on farm labor, football in their teens. Law enforcement from their twenties into their forties. Both used the police gym in the basement of the station three days a week. Thurman lifted heavy to maintain his Michelin Man physique, keep up with a county-fair-queen wife, two kids, while Whalen lifted medium to light, keeping his striated appearance, looked in his early forties but held the age of fifty and held it well. His ex-wife had remarried a state trooper years ago. They'd no kids.

Thurman's chest flexed between the cotton of his tan T-shirt and crossed arms, said, "Be the logical guess."

Whalen sipped the coffee remaining in his mug and asked, "What about the brass casing?"

"Same as those found at the house fire down in Amsterdam. Same prints but no hits in the criminal data base."

Pushing his hand over stubbled, military-kept hair, Whalen muttered, "Son of a bitch."

Thurman had more. "Most likely it's a male and female."

A hint of hope brightened Whalen's walnut eyes, and he asked, "Why you say that?"

"Two sets of footprints match both scenes. Size thirteen boot and size six. Same imprints was found on Eldon's kitchen tile. Had a soil match from Amsterdam. Also, bruises on Eldon's face are consistent with being beat by a big-ass set of knuckles. No female'd have those mitts wearing a size six."

"Small-framed woman."

"That's my logic. Plus, swab tests come back matching ejaculate from a female, unknown. And a male, Eldon. The dumb bastard was getting fucked when some gal decided to shoot him just before he wasted his glue."

"Twisted bitch," Whalen concluded.

Thurman shook his head. "Not your average holster chaser. How the interview with the Chinaman go?"

Whalen exhaled with disgust. "He's clean. Eldon owed him for some bets is the reason he stopped at the pharmacy. He called it business. Regardless, Mr. Zhong got an alibi. Can't touch that bastard. I visited the Leavenworth Tavern, Poe gave nothing. Stopped and talked to Flat and Beatle's pal Ned. He ain't spoke with them in a while. So he says."

Thurman said, "Keep a tab on him. At least we's pretty certain it's a man and woman."

Whalen leaned back, bent his corded arms behind his head. "It's been well past a week since we got the call on the house fire, found Beatle and Flat. I can either wait for another fire or pray for a poached body. Or—"

Thurman cut in, sitting down on Whalen's desk and leaning forward. "You thought about cruising back roads, checking abandoned houses in the county for squatting meth cooks?"

Whalen lowered his hands from behind his head, pushed himself up from his desk, reached for his hat, and said, "That's a damn good idea."

●

Fingers lined with gold-nugget rings and tipped by buffed nails laid two photos on the jade table that sat in a numb-gray basement. Slid them to the man on the other side.

The man sliding over the photos needed to find two people. His source told him that these people squatted in abandoned farm houses, cooked and sold meth. The man wanted to get his money back from a pharmacist who owed him an uncollected debt.

The manicured man's voice was direct. He stared into the other man's eyes, which sat like tadpoles behind thick glass. The other man picked up the photos. Took in the details of a man and woman. He wanted to know what had happened to the man's face.

The manicured man told him that the man in the photo had had a chainsaw accident. Used to own a logging business. Now he was the best meth cook around the county. Went by the nickname of Chainsaw Angus.

The tadpole-eyed man smirked, slid the photos into the breast pocket of his white short-sleeved button up. He had on each inner forearm a tattoo that signified his tutelage in a faraway school. A monkey branded his right. A snake branded his left. Mr. Zhong, he knew, had the same tattoos under his sleeves.

The tadpole-eyed man asked Mr. Zhong where he needed to start looking for this Chainsaw Angus.

Mr. Zhong owned five Chinese restaurants in six counties. Had come straight off the boat from the Fukien province. Turned the small amount of family money he'd had into a small profit. Used his businesses as fronts for his illegal bookie operation. He'd never lost a dollar. Always collected what was owed. Eldon was still delinquent.

Mr. Zhong told the tadpole-eyed man that his sources had reported the female used to run with two brothers now dead. They'd frequented a place of drink called the Leavenworth Tavern.

The tadpole-eyed man tipped his bowl-shaped head of hair forward. Then back. Raw light from the ceiling caught his face, highlighted the putty-like scars from years of offensive training as a boy. The knuckles of each hand were flat as the wood and bamboo he'd conditioned them against years ago. His forearms and shins were the same. Years of bones being pounded. Nerve endings numbed. Conditioned into steel.

His name was Fu Xi. Named after one of China's cultural heroes, the possible inventor of the eight trigrams for the *I Ching*, the Book of Changes. Mr. Zhong had brought Fu out of China. Now Mr. Zhong paid Fu to clean up his delinquent dilemmas when no other solution was plausible.

Fu slid his small frame from the red chair in which he'd sat. Stood with shirt tucked into pressed brown dress slacks. A leather belt around his waist. Slip-on loafers over his feet. He offered his free hand before Mr. Zhong left Fu's basement chamber, a makeshift monastery where he'd taught secretly out in the wilds of Harrison County. They shook.

Mr. Zhong paused, then told Fu that when he arrived at the tavern, his sources told him he'd need to speak with a bartender by the name of Poe. That he was a man that knew more than he let on. He was not an ignorant man, though he pretended to be.

10

In the passing hours of daylight and dark, Liz and Ned lay unbathed. Three days of chemical sweat. Cotton-mouth kisses and sandpaper tongues taking turns within each other's nether regions. Breaking for bumps of the man-made powder, chased with swigs of bourbon, bottles of Bud, cans of Natural Light.

They crashed in the cold, air-conditioned interior of Ned's tin shack. Cardboard blinds blocked light from the southern Indiana heat outside. Condensate beaded on the glass. Their chalky outlines lay intertwined like albino anacondas nesting.

Wednesday evening, Ned and Liz scrubbed the dead skin of the three-day binge from their flesh. Packed the meth in Liz's rucksack along with Angus's .45. Hit the road to Orange County in Ned's old Chevy. They purchased a sack of greasy burgers for the long ride. Washed them down with two black coffees. No AC. Windows rolled down. Clear blue daylight burning moisture from their eyes, turning their skin sticky once again.

Liz told Ned, "Sure could use a bump."

Ned gritted, "Gotta wait, unload some of it."

"Just a bump."

"Bit—" Ned stopped his words short. "We gotta wait."

Liz paused. Asked herself, This toothless fuck was about to call her a bitch? The dope was hers. He'd be bone on pavement he didn't watch it. She asked, "Where you say we's going?"

"The sticks down in Orange County. Guy I know named Pete, he and his brother Lang run a tavern down there. Pete's supposed to have set us up a deal 'fore we hit the 'Brook."

Liz questioned, "Brook?"

Ned said, "Donnybrook."

"Who the shit's he?"

"Not a he, a fight. Bare-knuckle free-for-all. Us fighters love our rush in any form 'fore we meet in the ring."

"Fighters? We selling crank to buncha' scrappers?"

"Pretty much the idea. There's a big crowd. Lot of betting goes on. Food. Booze. Good place to swonder your crank. It's like a Dead concert with fists."

Liz's eyes blew up like large pelts of hail. "How much we gonna make?"

"Handful of cash. Enough crank left over to drop out for a week or better after. That was the deal. Take out your old man. Help you sell this dope for half the split, samplings of your sours and the crank."

Liz shook her head, said, "He wasn't my old man. He was my goddamn crazy-as-shit brother. Used to be a fighter."

"No shit, well, he's home to fly larvae now. What was his name?"

"Angus, Chainsaw Angus."

Ned swelled up, offered his jack-o'-lantern smile. "Son of a bitch, I took out a legend."

•

Gravel had dragged Angus to the room where he and Liz had slept. Where walls of pasted vinyl curled and peeled. Wooden windowsills were weathered and musted, and with its rings of syrupy stains, the ceiling looked as if someone'd held a tobacco spitting contest. Twice a day Gravel brought a tin bucket of water, scrubbed the frayed mess of unstitched brawn with lye soap. Patted the moisture and rusty fluid from it. Dressed the wound with patches of linen cut from his sister's and mother's dresses that hung from a closet in the upstairs. When Angus had come around, the beast of a young man bared a palm into his chest. Stuttered his words of, "Y-you st-stay."

To wield the pain, Angus told the malignant shape of man to find the clear orange prescription bottle that lay in his ruck of clothing. And he had. Removing the lid, Angus had chased Vicodin with water, keeping the pain at bay.

Gravel had collected rabbits from his traps and sling-shot squirrel from trees for food. Gutted the insides, skinned them of fur and cleaned the meat, then fired the game along with potatoes for nourishment, fed Angus and himself along with roots he'd collected and dried during the previous spring, placed in a kettle of water, heated over embers and boiled the yellow to release its healing elements. He'd brought Angus back to a world where time was simple. Not many words were exchanged as food was chewed and eyes wandered about and the two men felt each other out. Angus would say, "Ain't half bad."

And as days passed Gravel felt some form of symbolism take shape. As though he'd lived with the purpose of the land and the land alone, but now that he had the land and another form to care for other than himself, he'd a much larger role in his daily existence.

Now, Angus sat shirtless in the disheveled kitchen, staring out the screen door. His strength was where it needed to be. The Vicodin keeping his pain at bay. One thought lingered, like the names engraved in roman script on his pallid body. GOTHIC IRIS, RAZORED CLINT, and ALI SQUIRES lined his forty-year-old pecs. MARVIN, ISRAEL, and JUNIS inked into his right shoulder. Names of fallen men. That thought was, Liz would go down.

A cigarette dangled from his lip. Smoke waved up into his nose, irritated his eyes. Problem was, Angus had no idea where Liz was.

He watched evening daylight burn through the mesh. A figure came from the distance up by the barn. This Gravel was some kind of ugly with his dress, boots, and split-tongue speech, but he'd nursed Angus's old roadkill ass back to the living.

Angus thought about blood being specked. Blotted onto a faded and curled surface. Thought about sharp edges. Flat knuckles. Openings 9 mm in size exhausting a person's insides.

He pulled on the Pall Mall. Exhaled. Asked himself, where would that nappy-headed bitch go with this sour-mouthed Ned? Man who had pulled the trigger. Had a piss-poor aim.

Gravel's shape was coming nearer and nearer, he looked to have supper in his one hand and something pointed in the other.

Angus closed his eyes. Leaned his head back. Anger jackhammered his thoughts. Creating a pain so deep his face went numb. He'd survived their murder plot. Had to get his dope back. Implement what Liz and Ned had failed to achieve—kill him.

The Vicodin churned his stomach. He needed solid food. Took a final pull on the smoke. Pushed himself to his feet. Needed some fresh air. His eyes steadied on the table, focused on the hard pack of red Pall Malls that lay open next to his car keys. A break of light ignited from within, seeded his mind with where Liz'd gone several nights back before his murder. He said, "Leavenworth Tavern."

Going into the back room where he'd slept, he pulled a shirt over his body, his wound dressed and scabbing beneath the ragged cotton. Grabbing his ruck, he listened to the door unbar, then the spring slam it into the jamb. He'd need to find some 9-mm shells. Then go talk to someone about a bitch in heat running with a mutt named Ned. Find them. Get his shit back. Leave them worse than they had left him. Place 'em deep into the earth.

In the kitchen, Gravel stood over the sink, turned with a mess of blood and a skinner in his hand. He'd a look of horrified surprise. "Wh-wh-what are y-you . . . do-do-doin'?"

"Movin' on."

Angus kneeled down, reached beneath the slab of kitchen table with his right. Grabbed for the 9-mm Taruas he'd duct-taped beneath it for an emergency. He ripped it from the table. Next thing he heard was the clank of steel hitting the sink and a shriek, "N-no!" Felt a hand grip and tug at his shoulder. "Y-you c-can't leave."

Angus eyed Gravel, whose retinas swelled and shrank with confused hurt, and told him, "Fuck I can't." He backed away from him.

Gravel thought of his father, thought of the bond he'd destroyed, something Gravel was building again after all of these years, nursing and caring for this soul so similar to him, his damaged appearance, then he stared at the pistol and said, "No . . . g-guns. H-hate . . . guns." And he came at Angus, reached for the 9 mm in his hand, the big wad of a human squeezed Angus's hand and the two men struggled for control of the gun. Angus's finger fell into place, he locked his jaws, strained and pressed the barrel into Gravel's gut, and without a second thought he tugged the trigger more than once.

Brass bounced hot. Blood pounded even hotter from Gravel's gut. He fell backward into the counter. Glancing down at the scatter of pulp and back at the pearl-eyed man, shocked and betrayed by this person he'd catered for like his own kin. A piercing whine of confusion belched from his mouth. Head twisting unorthodox from side to side, he slid down the cabinet, onto the exact spot he'd found Angus. Where Gravel's father had stood that day his family attained to no more.

Angus pushed the hot gun down into his waistband.

Grabbed his keys and pack of smokes off the table. Turned to Gravel, who patted at the heat flooding from his stomach, a lost look in his eyes. But Angus did not concede his actions of betrayal. He only said, "There's a gamble to everything one does in this life. Always a winner and a loser. Not sure of my role, but I know yours."

Out the screen door and into the oncoming evening Angus went. Down the creek-rock steps to his Pinto. The engine fired. He put it into reverse. Backed up. Put it into drive. Took off down the road like a vampire anticipating nightfall, muttering, "Coming to get you, bitch."

•

Pete waited with long arms vining from a faded, military-green Buckmasters T-shirt. Rested them on the nicked hardwood of Cur's Watering Hole, a tavern he and his brother owned. Sold some beer and some whiskey. Dealt meth and marijuana to customers. Hosted bare-knuckle fights in a dirt pit out back. Ran side bets and a cover charge. And every August, along with their cousin Poe, directed new onlookers and fighters through Harrison and Orange County to Bellmont McGill's Donnybrook.

All around Pete, men and women sat at tables made from large wooden spools that once held electric wire. Canning jars of golden brew and single shots of brown in front of them. Mouths spewing delinquent clatter. Pete's bartending older brother, Lang, watched the male and female enter Cur's, leaned on the other side of the bar in front of Pete, whispered, "You called them yet?"

"They're waiting like turkey hunters in a blind."

Lang warned Pete, "Watch your ass. Know that son of a bitch is spiny."

Pete nodded. Mouthed back, "I got it."

Lang walked to the other end of the bar. A hand met Pete's shoulder. He turned his peach-fuzzed chin into Ned's face and said, "Look what the Orange County sewage department shit out."

Ned offered, "If you ain't the stain on a raped heifer's bedsheet, don't know who is."

Pete skipped Liz's head of hair, worked his way down over her chest, then went back to her face. Complimented her with, "By God if you ain't the sweetest thing since strawberries dipped in sugar." Wiped his palm over ragged jeans, offered a hand. Told Liz, "Name's Peter, but everyone calls me Pete."

Liz met his hand with her own, returned a shithouse grin, said, "Hear you take more peter than you give."

Pete's pitted face burned like a candy apple and he mock-laughed. This was the best piece of ass he'd seen Ned run with, easy.

Ned popped the back of Liz's head with his hand, said, "Enough eye-fucking him." Looking around the room, he asked Pete, "Who's the people we selling some crank to?"

Pete pulled a crumpled piece of paper from his front pocket. His index and middle finger offered it. "Here's the directions. They's waiting down the road a spell."

Ned wrinkled his scar-tissue brows, asked, "You ain't going?"

Pete grabbed his Miller High Life from the bar, took a

swig, swallowed, said, "Naw, gotta give Lang a hand. But go 'head. They know you's coming."

•

Elbow heard the knock at the door. Hollered, "Don't be shy, get your ass on in here." The door opened and in walked Liz and Ned. The dank waft of the house's interior pricked the inside of their noses. Made them want to spit pieces of the burgers they'd washed down earlier.

Across from them, Elbow stood barefoot on a shag carpet that'd lost its vanilla tint to spots of his and his brother Dodge's spilt beers. A black-and-white floor-model TV sat over against a wall. Dodge sat in an electric wheelchair off behind Elbow, one hand wrapped about his Pabst Blue Ribbon, his other pinching his crotch. His eyes were two bored-out barrels aiming at Liz's chest.

Ned wanted to get this deal done quick. Wanted out of a home that stank of more rot than his own. Told the two, "The price is a hundred dollars per gram. So how much you wanna procure?"

Elbow rubbed the chest of his Lucky Charms T-shirt. Puckered a pair of tobacco worm lips covered in white donut powder. Then pushed a hand down the front of his green nylon gym shorts, let the thumb wiggle over the hem. His fingertips tickled the bulge that pressed beneath the fabric like a large spider under a dryer sheet. He twisted his neck over his right shoulder to the disabled war veteran, his mousy voice asking, "How much you wanna spend, brother Dodge?"

83

Dodge lifted the can of PBR to his lips. Made a slurping sound that his thorny Adam's apple moved with. Lowered the can and belched. Moved his eyes from Liz to Ned, asked, "How much you got?"

Ned's nerves were rattled by the dead pierce in Dodge's eyes, and in a sarcastic tone he said, "Plenty more than you can likely afford, crip."

Dodge returned a smirk and said, "Why don't you go get us a thousand dollars' worth, pyorrhea-mouth."

Ned kept his eyes on the two brothers, clenched his fist, said, "Liz, go out to the truck, get these dingleberries they crank."

"No!" Dodge spit. "The girl can stay. You go get the fucking crank!"

Ned hesitated, then turned around, twisted the doorknob. Went out the door. Liz took in the desert camouflage pattern of Dodge's legs that sat useless, his feet covered by a pair of black Velcroed tennis shoes. He had on a gray T-shirt with stains across wide letters that spelled ARMY. His face was sharp-boned, jaundice-tanned, cactus-stubbled, topped with a head of mahogany hair, the ends of which looked singed by flame.

Liz broke the uncomfortable silence, asked, "Guess you's in the army?"

Elbow's entire hand disappeared down his gym shorts.

Dodge told Liz, "Two fucking years in Iraq. Draw a pension now till our pagan lord lets me rot in a box forged by Chink hands that'll read MADE IN THE USA."

Elbow's wormy knees began to bend while he pushed his lower back forward, thrusting his crotch up like he was humping the air. His hand still lost down his shorts, gripping the bulge.

Liz asked, "That what happened to your legs?"

Elbow began opening and closing his mouth in a stiff yawn, lip-syncing a Slayer tune, "Reign in Blood," that only he heard. His other hand balled into a fist and punched at the ceiling while he dry-humped the air.

Cake-batter-thick spittle flew from the corners of Dodge's mouth as he hollered, "You think happen to my legs, you stupid cunt? Goddamned fucking Hummer hit a IED!"

Liz got red-faced, skipped the lighting of the fuse and ignited with, "You inbred paraplegic fuck! I didn't tell you to go over there. Same as I didn't name you after a goddamned truck maker."

Dodge had started to growl when Ned stepped back into the small house, several clear baggies of ghost-white crystal in hand.

"Quit the fucking hollering," said Ned. "I got your shit right here. Now cough up the grand of spare change."

Elbow lowered his left hand from the air, pulled his right hand from his gym shorts, bringing that big hard bulge with it. Aimed it at Liz and Ned. It was an onyx .38 handgun, and he told them, "Had to be sure you had the shit. Now we take the whole mess of what you got out yonder for free. After your nappy-headed bitch gets on her knees, takes that shirt of hers off. Lets me service them fun sacks while she tastes my ugly stick."

11

Purcell pulled two fishing rods from the rusty nails he'd driven into the studs years ago. Grabbed his tackle box from a dust-deviled shelf, stepped from the wilted shed that was the color of pus, and started down the path to his johnboat. He kept it beached next to the Ohio River. He'd no idea how long he'd wait. How any of it would happen. He just knew that Jarhead would come from the wooded hillside. Stray from Alonzo's place. For reasons he could only imagine. Those that corralled at Alonzo's place were any and all manner of lowdown, without morals. Seeking sickness and carnage. Some said he'd tried to bring young girls from foreign lands, to sell their skin. Entertain those that were into the puerility.

He lay his gear in the chipped boat and the sooty water splashed. Busted tree limbs, beer, and oil cans lay scattered along mushy earth. Purcell pushed the boat into the water, waded in until the wet lined the top of his rubber boots, and with the sun beating down on him he hopped in the boat. Pulled the cord on the small motor, glanced down the flanks of the river, checking for barges so he could cross to the other side, knowing the heat he felt wetting his skin beneath his clothing was nothing compared to what was soon to come.

•

Cans of gasoline surrounded Jarhead. He ran one hand through his sweaty locks. Thought about those lights from a few nights back. The truck's gas pedal to the floor. The red-and-blue flashes that had opened the night. He took the back-road curves not knowing his way. But outrunning them.

Now, Jarhead stood in a rusted tin garage, a grease-smudged rotary phone held to his ear, thumbing a creased and worn picture of Tammy and the boys. He hadn't spoken to them in days, missed the boys watching him skip rope in the dirt yard and work the heavy bag in the late evenings. They'd clap their tiny hands in amusement. After training he bathed them and tucked them into bed for sleep. Showered, then went into his bedroom, wrapped his arms around Tammy's warm innocence.

He'd needed to let Tammy know he was okay. Make sure she and the boys were the same. Into the phone he asked, "Anyone hassle you?"

The female voice was feather-pillow-soft with worry. "Marshal Pike just wanted to know if I'd seen or heard from you. Wondered why you'd go and rob a gun shop for one grand. Not take a penny more and leave the shotgun."

"What'd you tell him?" Jarhead asked.

Tammy said, "Last I seen you the sun was rising. The kids was crying with shitty diapers."

Jarhead was restless and a bit worried. He hadn't beat on a bag nor run for conditioning since the robbery. He needed to expand his lungs. Feel some flesh give. Bring some hurt. He needed to make some tracks toward Orange County. And he wasn't real comfortable with what had happened a few nights back. Worried about the county officer he'd beat, the man he'd choked out, the cops he'd outrun. What if they'd gotten the plate number of the truck he'd fled the scene in with Tig? He told Tammy, "It'll be over soon."

Tammy asked, "Promise?"

"Promise. After this coming weekend I be the winner of the Donnybrook. I'll send someone for you and the babies."

Tig and his cousin had given him a place to rest his head, a spare room with a cot and soured sheets. In the night Jarhead heard a lot of men coming and going from the basement. But he ignored whatever it was they did besides siphoning fuel. They were his transportation to Orange County this evening.

"Why not you?" Tammy asked.

Jarhead told her, "Can't risk being seen in or near Hazard after what I done did. I win, none of that'll matter no way. Be more money than either of us ever did see in our lives."

Tammy got quiet. A child sneezed in the background. She asked, "What if you don't win? What if they's someone meaner and tougher than you? Then what we gonna do?"

There was always a *what if?*. Like the first time Jarhead threw a punch. What if that man hadn't seen him do it? Knock that other boy silly for bullying another. What if he'd not seen something in Jarhead? Taken him under his wing. Learned him how to fight. Throw a punch. An elbow. A knee. How to work his hips. Rotate and turn a fist. Where to hit and how to hit. The kidneys. The liver. Heart. How to take care of his body. Be confident, not cocky, like the man he'd never known. His real father. A marine who'd served in the Vietnam war and boxed in Puerto Rico. The man that his mother had nicknamed him after. She told him she'd left Miles before Johnny was born. That his real father, Miles Knox, spoke with the dead. Had a violent streak and a hankering for the bourbon. His mother had given him her maiden name, not his father's.

Johnny often wondered if Miles was alive or had passed away. He'd never tried to make contact. His mother had confessed all of this to him just days before the dark cloud hit and she'd committed suicide after his stepdaddy had passed from black lung.

"Honey," he said, "they is always someone meaner. But the smart fighter is the better fighter. I'll win. I've no other choice. Then I'll send someone for you."

Tammy questioned once more, "You promise?"

"I done told that I did."

"Wanna hear you say it again."

The gloom in Tammy's tone was killing him. He had to stay focused on their future, not her uncertain sadness.

"Promise." Jarhead changed the subject. "How our babies doing?"

Tammy's voice cheered up. "Little Caleb is getting the sneezes. Zeek is sleeping."

"How about you, got enough Oxycontin for your pains?"

Tammy had lower-back spasms from an uncle who'd raised her with knuckles, knees, and slats of busted pine to her body after her parents disappeared with the traveling fairs. From her childhood to adulthood, all she knew was pain. Till she met Jarhead. Who took her away. Paid the uncle a late-night visit. Made sure he'd never touch anything breathing again.

She said, "Yeah, but not enough to drown my worry for you."

She was so sweet it made her love tart, and that made Jarhead love her that much more.

A man's voice hollered, "Jarhead?"

He turned. Tig's cousin, Alonzo Conway, came into the dirt-floored, tin-sided garage carrying two red five-gallon gas containers. "Sorry, son, didn't know you's on the wire."

Jarhead told Tammy, "I gotta get. I'll call Sunday evening."

Tammy asked, "Who's that?"

"Alonzo. One of the guys helping me get to the Donnybrook. Love you."

"Love you."

Jarhead hung up the phone.

Alonzo owned a fifty-acre plot with a monstrous rundown farmhouse out in the sticks, along the Ohio River. He placed the gasoline-filled containers on the floor. Offered a hand to Jarhead. A cigarette hung from his lip. Ash fell as he spoke. "Wanna thank you again for helping Cousin Tig. Seeing as you won't take no cash, left something on your bunk in the house." Alonzo's fudge-tinted hair was wild and fatty in all directions. His skin was fiery red. Glowed with sweat beneath his T-shirt and jeans. He pulled the cigarette from his lip. Flipped it out the sliding tin doors behind him, onto the red clay. Winked an eye to Jarhead. Picked up the gas containers. Said, "Best hurry up yonder 'fore it gets cold." Walked to the rear of the garage.

In the house, floorboards gave and screeched under Jarhead's boots. He pushed the bedroom door open. A girl who appeared no older than a freshman in high school sat on his cot. Hands behind a head of hair the shade of pond mud, thick-bristled and shoulder-length. Her complexion was steam white. She had metallic hazel eyes outlined by Mötley Crüe mascara. She was Twizzler-lipped. Two bra-less mounds lumped beneath a V-neck Hanes cut low. Her flat belly with a thick-gauged piercing poked out above a pair of cutoff sweats. Her right leg bent at the knee. Left leg wrapped in a leather brace. Piece of steel attached to it ran down to a thick-heeled shoe. A matching shoe attired her right foot. She smiled, her teeth vanilla-tinted. "Where you get all this money?"

The Walmart sack of cash with Jarhead's clothing sat beside her.

Jarhead approached her. Said, "None of your worry." And grabbed the sack. Asked, "Who the shit are you?"

The girl smiled, said, "Mag Pie."

"The hell you want?"

"Whatever you want. I'm here for you saving Cousin Tig."

Jarhead started to laugh. "Girl, you're all of what— fifteen? I ain't into jail-bait snatch."

She lowered her hands to her knees. Pouted her lips. Batted her eyes. Then cupped both of the mounds under her shirt. Thumbs brushed back and forth, hardened her nipples. "I's seventeen. Can't you tell by the way I filled out? My sister Key Hole is fifteen. But she got a nicer set than I got."

Jarhead swallowed hard, told her, "Look, I've got me a proper female. Two kids. Mouths to feed. No interest in defying my woman's trust."

Mag Pie bent forward. Balanced herself. Stood up. Kick-stand limped toward Jarhead. Reached for his crotch. He slapped her hand away. She blushed. "Tig says you're a fighter. I like it rough."

Jarhead shook his head, told her, "Ain't interested."

She touched the leather brace on her leg. Fingered the metal. "Is it 'cause of my noodle leg? No worry, I can take you some places that girl of yours never has."

Jarhead raised his voice. "I got no interest in fucking a kid. You need go on and get."

"The shit's going on in here?" Alonzo came into the room. Sweaty and fuel-scented.

"Your new friend don't wanna rub openings with me, Uncle. Says I too young."

Alonzo stared at Jarhead. "Is that so? Shit far, just tryin' to thank you for your services. Be awful rude you didn't give her a test ride."

Jarhead wanted to be even ruder, beat Alonzo's complexion into every shade of Life Savers candy. "I done told her, ain't interested in fucking no kid. Or any female other than my girl for that matter."

Alonzo said, "Girl like Mag's a hundred dollar a squirt. You can take the day with her for nothing."

Mag interrupted. "The day?"

93

Alonzo told her, "Figured you'd like a young buck instead of them wrinkled mule-dick farmers."

Jarhead grabbed Alonzo's arm, said, "She's seventeen, you sick fuck."

Alonzo jerked his arm away. Eye-fucked Jarhead, told him, "No man wants a wore-out section of puss. Younger the better. And no man touches and disrespects me in my own home."

Jarhead held his sack of cash tighter, said smoothly, "I best be going, make my way to the Donnybrook. I'm a fighter, gotta fight."

Alonzo stepped into Jarhead's face. "That's what you keep telling, so maybe we ought's find out if it's true."

Mag Pie chimed, "Should see all the cash he got in that there sack."

Alonzo glanced down to the blue plastic sack that hung weighted from Jarhead's left hand, asked, "You rob a bank or something? Tig tells that you's a helluva wheelman."

Jarhead's right hand clenched into a fist. Pressed the knuckles bone-white. His hips were already positioned to give Alonzo a quick beating, and he said, "Told you I's going to fight in the Donnybrook, and it cost a grand to fight."

Alonzo reached for the sack. Jarhead pulled it away. Came down hard with his head. Butted Alonzo's. Shifted his left hip back, came forward with a right uppercut. Alonzo fell backward, bumped into Mag Pie. His hands triangled around his face, and he shouted, "Watch out, little bitch!"

"You watch out, clown-footed fuck."

Jarhead stepped to the bedroom's doorway. Tig blocked

it. Bare-chested, pale, and bandaged. Announced, "Got a mess of trouble. They's four county cruisers out in the drive."

Down the hall a cop's fist pounded on the kitchen door. Alonzo told Tig, "Go get the guns."

12

Something scorched from the tarnished trailer lingered, littered the country air. Muddled voices rebounded from inside.

Whalen had searched ten abandoned houses in two days on various county back roads. Houses once white, weathered to gray. Roofs rotted. Busted windows and doors opening to yellowed and peeled wallpaper. Gutted trucks and tractors in yards of knee-high ragweed. But no trace of meth cooks, only disregarded memories.

He'd followed the mudded path once graveled. No mailbox at the end of the drive. Seen two four-wheelers parked up by a woodshed. Miniature wooden wagon attached to one of them. White bags of trash piled on the back. Someone was living inside the trailer. Whalen had watched several swells of gray rat run to and from it.

He now sat in his cruiser, engine off, window down, surrounded by briars and ivy. Watched the trailer. Being this deep into the seclusion of the backwoods made Whalen think about his secret and the girls who were no more. The boy he'd not visited in quite a while. Wouldn't be visiting him today, he thought, grabbing his radio.

Keying it, he said, "Tanner, this is two."

"Go 'head, two."

"I'm down past Blue Hole at the old Farnsley place. Gonna investigate a suspicious smell coming from the trailer. Possible meth lab. Send Officer Meadows down here ASAP just in case. Get a state boy on standby."

"Copy."

Whalen stepped from the cruiser slow. Kept his eyes on the cardboard that replaced the broken windows. Searched for peepholes with guarding eyes. Focused on the front door that he approached with his gun removed from its holster. Safety off. Stopping within earshot of the front door, he smelled rot, piss, objects soured, and burning chemical. The muddled voices from inside became clear.

A female hollered, "Son of a bitch, I kill you!"

"Bitch, get your mask on!" Sounded as though a man was yelling through a foam Dixie cup.

The female said, "Let me have a whiff."

The male threatened, "I done telling you." Followed by a sound that echoed like a cleaver slamming through thick cuts of meat. Then a thud that shook the trailer.

Kneeling down, Whalen positioned his Glock in his right hand. He reached up, wrapped his left hand around the doorknob, turned it slow, made sure it wasn't locked. Swallowed. Counted to three. Pushed the door open, stepped into the trailer.

His heart double-jabbed and right-crossed his chest. Burnt ammonia gagged his inhale. Moistened his eyes. Mixed with the sour waft of three kids on a red vinyl front seat pulled from a '77 Monte Carlo. Their unwashed hair clumped and matted. Shirts that matched their soiled bodies and mud-bogged underwear. Their mouths and cheeks textured the shade of liver.

Whalen aimed his Glock down at a female in a rayon nightgown trying to stand up from the floor of wadded paper. Empty plastic baggies. Coleman canisters. Everything flung in disarray.

She'd a twisted nest of hair the shade of water-contaminated engine oil. Her complexion was the hue of cottage cheese. Her braless sags pressed against her gown as she stood up. Scratches and buckeye bruises stretched about her ginseng-veined arms and legs. She screamed at Whalen, "The fuck you staring at, swine?"

Whalen demanded, "Show your hands!"

To Whalen's right, empty boxes of Sudafed and jugs of distilled water lined a kitchen counter where a man hovered over a stove, holding a wooden spoon. An orange flame heated liquid into bubbles within a clear glass bowl. The man's belly, chitlin-white and covered in mossy curled hair, peeked from beneath a T-shirt two sizes too small and rested over his red plaid pants. Black elastic straps ran over his bald head, securing a gas mask. Cylinders connected on each side of his mouth for Darth Vader–style breathing.

The man looked at Whalen, his eyes fogged behind two circles of Plexiglas. His muffled voice yelled, "Go 'head and shoot, watch us all flame up, porky."

Whalen told him, "Step away from the stove."

The woman hollered, "He don't have to do shit! Can't you see we's cooking?"

Whalen had a cockfight in his chest and told her, "Lady, shut your mouth! Sir, step away from the fucking stove!"

In his Darth Vader tone, the man said, "Don't talk that way to my wife. Got kids in the house."

Losing his patience, Whalen said, "Sir—"

Before Whalen could react, the female grabbed at the kitchen counter. Turned. Lunged Lizzy Borden–style at him. Whalen raised his left arm to block the oncoming blur. Took a gash from the blade of a butcher knife. Yelled, "Shit!"

He hooked his left hand around the woman's wrist. Kept the knife controlled. Pounded the butt of his Glock down onto her forehead. She dropped to her knees along with the knife. Whalen released her wrist. The woman screamed, "You fuck!"

Quivering like the adrenaline cooking on the stove, the man rushed Whalen. Whalen fired a round into the man's right thigh. The female hollered, "No!" The man fell forward onto Whalen. From the car seat in the living room the kids started barking like hounds on a coon trail. Then Whalen felt pain stab into his left thigh. Gritted out, "Dammit!" The man pushed his weight against Whalen, grabbed for his gun. Whalen glanced down. The woman was on her knees. She grabbed the butcher knife again, drove it into Whalen's leg. While Whalen wrestled the man for control of the gun, the lady hollered for the kids. "You little bastards get in here, help your mother and father!"

Whalen held tight to the Glock. The man had both hands wrapped on top of Whalen's, prying and pulling at his grip. Then the woman stood up. Bear-hugged and pushed at Whalen and her husband. Whalen backpedaled, lost his footing. His back hit the floor. The weight of the man and woman slammed down on top of him. Took his wind. Fatigue set in. Whalen huffed for air, didn't know how much longer he could keep control of the gun, fight the man and woman. Then he felt three sets of teeth dig into his shin and thigh, gnawing like rabid hounds.

•

Liz's knees mashed into pasty fibers. Elbow balled his right hand into her budded cords of hair. His left hand pressed the .38 into Ned. Who stood with his hands raised and back turned to the menace he'd dealt them into.

Elbow's tongue circled his lips, and he told Liz, "Don't act as though you never had rug burn on them knees."

Liz's eyes had no other view aside from what was before her, the mound hidden behind the green fabric of Elbow's gym shorts.

To her left, Dodge sat in his wheelchair inhaling crank chased with gulps of PBR, screaming, "Go on, pull it out! Pull it out!"

Elbow forced Liz's face into his crotch. Liz dug her fingers into the backs of Elbow's shaggy thighs. Opened her mouth. Took all that she could fit: the tainted fabric of his shorts, the hard lump hidden behind it, and the taste of soured dairy.

Elbow slurped, "Oh yeah, baby, you know you want all of me."

Liz bit down onto as much as she could chew and pulled away.

Elbow's scream was electric. He released Liz's hair. Lowered the gun pointed at Ned's head.

Ned turned, hooked his left hand around Elbow's wrist. Grabbed the .38. Pulled it free. Stepped behind Elbow, swung a right hook into Elbow's head. Brought the butt of the .38 in his left hand down onto the opposite side of Elbow's skull. Elbow hit the floor.

Dodge sat in his wheelchair screaming, "Yeah! Get it! Get it! Beat his shit! Beat it!"

Liz wiped her mouth. Looked down at Elbow on the carpet. Both of his hands between his legs, his outline rounded into a ball of salivating wailing that rocked back and forth. Ned stepped past Liz to Dodge, pressed the gun to his head. "Where's the cash, you worm?"

Dodge's eyes were two cat claws tearing into Ned's, and he growled, "Eat shit."

Ned raised the gun, dented Dodge's face like an aluminum can. Dodge spat, "You sumbitch."

Ned turned to Liz. "We ain't leaving till we get paid. Go down the hall, see if you can find any cash in they bedroom. I got them."

Fed up, in her mind Liz called Ned everything from a piece of maggot shit to a living, breathing miscarriage as she followed the hallway to the first opening. A bathroom. Took in the porcelain toilet with a tangerine ringworm stain, matching sink, and mystery mold resurfacing the tub. Towels wadded on the floor. Empty toilet paper roll. Busted mirror. Said to herself, "This place is worse than Ned's."

Out of the bathroom, back down the hall, she entered

the only bedroom. Wood-framed bunk beds were pushed into a corner against the wall. Identical Raggedy Ann and Andy covers on top and bottom. Looked as though Dodge slept on the bottom, his name engraved in the bottom rail. Elbow's engraved in the top. Liz shook her head. "What the shit?"

Clothing mildewed in piles. Superhero action figures lined a bookshelf. Comic books were stacked with *Soldier of Fortune* mags on top of a dresser. Porn mags with big-breasted females sat bedside. Porn movie boxes lay scattered across the floor. Liz kicked through the array of filth, searched through a closet. Found an AR-15 assault rifle. A metal container of ammunition. A gun cleaning kit.

Looked between the mattresses. Then the dresser. Found some crusted condoms. A tub of Vaseline decorated with cock hairs. Boxes of latex gloves. Handcuffs. A .22 revolver. But no cash.

Back in the living room Ned asked, "Nothing?"

Liz shook her head. "Nothing of use. I'll check the freezer."

Ned looked dumbfounded. "Freezer?"

Liz said, "Folks I always knew either kept they money in a coffee can in the fridge or buried out in the yard."

The fridge was dirt brown, lined with superhero magnets and Scotch-taped Polaroids of nude women. Her hand wrapped around the handle. Dodge started driveling. "Stay out of there, you cunt!"

Inside the freezer, clear baggies held frosted shapes. Behind them sat a blue oxidized Maxwell House can. Liz pulled it out, knocked a few baggies to the linoleum.

Removed the lid. Glanced inside. Her eyes lit up, and she told Ned, "They's a wad in here big enough to gag a horse."

Ned grimaced, stepped over to Elbow. Kneeled down, laced his fingers into Elbow's Crisco locks. Pulled his head back, pressed the revolver into his dribbling eye, and asked, "Where's you supposed to meet Pete?"

•

The kids' teeth dug into Whalen's left side like ants hollowing into soil. Toxins boiled from the stove, engulfed the trailer, made it hard for Whalen to breathe. He held tight to his gun with both hands. The man pulled at his grip, his heart pounding against Whalen's chest, pumping the warm of his insides onto Whalen's pant leg.

The female pushed her Glock-swelled forehead into Whalen's face. Bared her burnt-grease teeth, ran her wide tongue over his cheek, into his ear, and grabbed for his crotch.

Whalen shuddered. Focused all his strength into his grip, pushed the gun into someone. Pulled the trigger. The loud pop deafened him. A muffled voice shouted, "Shit!" The man quit fighting for the gun. Whalen pulled the trigger again. Felt the woman's lips purse in his ear, her hand let go of his crotch. She rolled away from him. He released the gun with his left hand. Held on with his right. Slid his left hand down his side, felt a mouth clamp down onto his wrist. Ignored the pain. Pulled his mace free. Jerked his hand from the small mouth. Started spraying the mace down into the gnawing.

The kids fell back screaming with miniature coils of fist cranking into their eye sockets. Moisture fell from their eyes like condensate dripping from steamed glass.

Whalen pushed backward, away from the man and woman.

The man sat on the floor, leaned back against the stove. Chest fast expanding. Palm of one hand pressed into his leg. Forearm of his other holding the stomach of his T-shirt. Red pooled into a giant splotch.

The female lay on her back, both hands pressed into her chest, coughing violently. Mucus and blood erupting fountainlike from her mouth. The kids crawled and pushed up against her still rubbing their eyes, crying, "Mommy, Mommy!"

Whalen sat up next to the open trailer door, inhaling fresh air. He released the mace. His insides huffed on adrenaline. Everything attached to his left side pounded with hurt. He held his Glock in the air, ready to shoot anyone who shadowed in his direction.

Whalen heard tires stop outside the open door. A door slam. Bark of radio-static voices. Officer Meadows stepped through the trailer door, bent down to Whalen, mouthed, "Shit!"

Whalen gasped, "Took you long enough." Lowered his gun.

The toxic smell from the kitchen stove flamed Meadows's sight. He told Whalen, "Don't fucking move." Keyed the mic clipped to his shoulder. Said, "Tanner, this is four. Got us a situation out here at the Farnsley place. Deputy Sheriff Whalen has been stabbed." Meadows glanced at the man and woman with the crying kids and back at Whalen. "Appears two suspects have been shot, still breathing, kids sprayed by mace, gonna need a ambulance and—"

Whalen saw a hint of movement. The man had made it to his feet. Picked up the clear glass bowl from the stove without gloves. Whalen could smell the bare flesh of the man's hands burning as the man tossed the heated liquid onto Meadows. Whalen rolled to his right. Unloaded his firearm on the man. Who dropped the glass bowl. Fell against the stove. Meadows's screams ruptured the trailer's interior.

13

Radio static crackled through the kitchen door. Down the hallway from the kitchen, Tig handed a .30-30 with a scope to Alonzo along with a box of ammunition. Alonzo told Mag Pie, "Get your beaver tail down in the basement with the others." She gimped to a door down the hall. Opened it and disappeared with a clicking sound behind her.

Outside the kitchen door, a shadowed county officer got tired of waiting. Decided, Fuck procedure. Turned the doorknob. Alonzo stepped fast up the hallway. Daylight breathed through the kitchen door. Alonzo pressed the side of his right shoulder against the hallway wall where it opened up into the unlit kitchen. Shouldered the rifle. Raised the barrel.

Back down the hallway, Tig handed a black-plated .45 Tauras to Jarhead. He hefted its weight. "What the shit you want me to do with this?"

Tig held out a box of shells. "Best use it you wanna live."

Jarhead tucked the pistol down into his waistband. Took the shells. Placed them in the Walmart sack. "You's crazy."

In the kitchen, the officer stood in the doorway. One

hand rested on his side, touching his holstered handgun. Hollered, "Alonzo Conway, Meade County Police Department!" as he took in the kitchen. Lights off. Wooden table. Chairs pushed beneath. Rusted pearl fridge. Water-damaged wood floor. Counter filled with empty cans of Miller High Life, half gallon of Old Crow. Then the dark hallway. He stepped forward, squinted his eyes. Saw the barrel pointed at him too late. Alonzo said, "Nosy piece of bacon."

A deafening blast erupted from the .30-30's barrel. Half the officer's face opened. He stutter-stepped backward, fell out the doorway. His body spread out like a puppy-soiled rug on the porch, wet and spotted.

The gunshot buckled Jarhead, who watched Tig step toward the kitchen. Said, "The shit! Came too far to get caught. This ain't my quarrel." Raced down the hallway in the opposite direction, opening doors to other rooms in the old house, searching for a back door.

Tig limped into the kitchen with a high-powered rifle, a box of shells. Alonzo pushed the kitchen door closed. Gunshots started to rattle the wood siding of the farm-house. Glass busted from windows. Alonzo stuck the rifle out the broken glass of the door. Through the rifle's scope, he eyed the cops hunkered over the tops of their vehicles like pond turtles on a log, shotguns and pistols flashing rounds off at his house.

None of the windows in the house had a screen. Just wood framed around glass. Tig had done lifted the window above the kitchen sink. Shouldered his rifle. Yelled over the gunfire to Alonzo, "How many you count?"

Alonzo yelled, "Looks to be nine. Ten is littered on our porch with his final thoughts. The shit's Jarhead?"

The walls of the kitchen snapped drywall dust and Tig yelled, "Thought he's behind me."

Alonzo looked as though he'd chewed and swallowed a piece of spoiled meat, and he yelled, "Gutless swine, probably took to the woods! He'll get his! Just like these pork holsters gonna get theirs!"

Down the hallway Jarhead entered a back bedroom. Closed the door behind him. Stared at bedsheets wadded upon a bare mattress. Boxers, jeans, and T-shirts obscuring the hardwood floor's surface. Empty cigarette boxes strewn and stubbed-out butts ashed across the top of a scuffed dresser and nightstand. Jarhead said to himself, "What a fucking shit box."

He stepped across the clothes through a wood-framed screen door on the far side of the room and out onto a small concrete porch. Looked out into a graveyard of rusted engines and rubber tires scattered atop patches of grass, dirt, and rock that bordered acres and acres of woods.

Then he smelt stale-coffee words behind the pistol that pressed into his temple, telling him, "Don't fucking move!"

Outside, the gunfire ceased. In the driveway, a police officer stood cinnamon-faced between his cruiser and his open door, held up his hand, mouthed, "Hold your damn fire!"

Officers reloaded their weapons. The one who held up his hand lowered it, pulled a radio mic from inside his cruiser. Keyed it. His words blasted through the megaphone speaker attached to the top of his car. "Alonzo Conway, this is Deputy Sheriff Burnham. Got a warrant for you and your cousin for trafficking in underage prostitution, selling siphoned fuel, and—"

Alonzo didn't let Burnham finish. Tugged the trigger. Watched Burnham's shoulder segment through the high-powered rifle's scope.

Tig eyed the carnage, hollered, "Damn, that piece of pork's been pulled."

Police officers started pumping rounds of lead back at the farmhouse.

Tig pulled the bolt action back. Dropped an empty brass to the floor. Levered a fresh round into the chamber. Looked through the rifle's scope. Repeated with fresh rounds. Worked his way to the left, cutting through glass, steel, and skin.

Alonzo's right thigh blew out red. He fell back. Screamed, "Fuck!" Held the .30-30 in his left hand. Pressed his right hand into his thigh. Red poured through his fingers. He dropped the .30-30, twisted, reached above his head, patted the counter. Feeling for a rag or towel. Something to dam the flow.

Tig turned, his ears ringing, and looked at the blood running from Alonzo's leg. The soiled hand patting the counter. While the repetitive rounds of gunfire sounded like a car backfiring, boring out the kitchen.

He dropped to the floor. Pushed his back into the cabinets. Pulled the small clip from his rifle. Fingered shells from the box of ammunition into the rifle's clip. Tasted the drywall- and wood-splintered air. Looked to Alonzo. "What now?"

Alonzo's face was condensate on a cold faucet. He mouthed, "Gas tanks. Aim for the cruisers' gas tanks."

Out back of the house, the county cop told Jarhead, "Get your hands up where I can see them." Jarhead started to raise his hands. Turned his right hand palm up, popped the underside of the county cop's right forearm, knocked the gun from his grip. The gun bounced out into the yard. Jarhead came full circle with the Walmart sack of money, clothes, and box of ammunition in his left fist leading the turn, hammering into the county cop's face. He palmed the cop with his free hand, pushing him backward off the concrete porch. The cop's back hit the ground. Knocked the air from his lungs.

Jarhead leaped from the concrete slab, over the cop, ran through the maze of engines and tires and into the woods with the sound of firecrackers lighting up the air behind him. His heart pumped in his ears; moisture seeded his body. Tree limbs whipped and scratched at his face and arms. Twigs cracked beneath him till he jumped a rotted tree, didn't land on his feet but spiraled down a steep decline of tree, rock, and loose earth.

•

When Pete entered Elbow and Dodge's house like they'd agreed, to split the crank and watch the brothers have their way with Ned and Liz, the butt of Elbow's .38 cracked the rear of his skull. Made his eyes wilt and his knees buckle.

From the carpet, Pete rubbed his head, looked to Ned,

and insulted him with "Three-teeth fuck. You owe me and—"

Ned grinned. "Owe you shit."

Ned motioned Pete to his feet to sit on the lumpy couch next to Elbow, who still sat holding his crotch, whimpering and slurping mucus.

Pete said, "Robbed us at the bar when everyone was gone few months back. We know'd it was you come in with a wad cutter, wearing that silly-ass Power Rangers mask."

Ned hollered, "Shut your hole! You all fixing to get what you deserve. Try and take my dope, fuck my woman."

Ned had double-crossed Pete. Liz understood what he was saying. Who the shit would wear a Power Ranger's mask to rob a bar? He wouldn't get a chance to double her. She'd be sure of that when they got to the Donnybrook. Plenty of others be doing favors for a piece of what she had. Liz looked at Ned. "Ain't just your dope."

Ned exhaled from his nose, said, "You know what I mean." He motioned with the gun. "Go see if you can find some molasses up in them cabinets they got in the kitchen."

Pete glanced to Liz, told her, "Don't be trusting this crooked piece of tin. He'll steal your crank, leave you like a two-dollar whore."

Ned hollered, "Told you, shut your hole!"

Pretending to ignore Pete, Liz held confusion on her face. "Molasses?"

Ned's face pressed wrinkles of hate from his forehead down onto his eyes, and he said, "Bitch, don't question me. Go look."

The shit he think he is? Liz thought. Done brought his

hand to the back of her head when they met Pete. Liz had Angus's piece. Ned kept throwing his words around, she'd augment his mouth to a discomforting width.

In the kitchen, Liz didn't find molasses. But reached for something else.

"Honey bear work?"

From beside the couch, Dodge hollered, "Don't be fucking with my sweets."

"Goddammit, done told you all to shut up," Ned said as he raised the revolver. He squeezed the trigger, opened Dodge's right shin. Dodge just sat there. Hollered, "Dumbass, I's cripple. Can't feel my fucking legs."

Ned shook his head, held the gun on Elbow and Pete, told them, "You two shit-sacks take off your clothes."

Each spoke with confusion. "The hell for?"

Ned told them, " 'Cause I got the gun. Undress."

Both men stood up. Elbow twitched, nearly fell over pulling his Lucky Charms T-shirt over his head. Then he dropped his stretchy gym shorts. Saggy lemon-colored nut huggers that should've been white. Pete pulled off his boots. Stood up, unbuckled his belt, said, "You's about the queerest son of a bitch I ever did see. Gonna steal her shit. Know you will. Probably done skimmed a pinch here and there already."

Ned got flush-faced, screamed, "Shut up!"

Liz held the bottle of honey, wondered if he had been skimming. How much.

Undressed, each man was talcum-fleshed. Bruised and scabbed. Pete was wiry and knotted. Elbow was Ethiopian-thin, his bones riding tight under his flesh from tweaking, from not eating and sleeping. He'd cuts up and down his inner thigh like stretch marks. Ned motioned them over next to Dodge. Elbow asked, "Why ain't he got to get naked?"

Ned couldn't believe this shit. Told Elbow, " 'Cause he don't, that's why."

Pete stood ass-and-balls bare beside Elbow and said, " 'Cause this crank-filching queer don't go for the handicapped."

Ned yelled at Liz, "Give me that honey. Go to the truck, get that roll of duct tape from the glove box."

Liz sized up the men and their fleshiness, winked at Pete and the girth of his third leg, and asked Ned, "Why?"

Ned balled the fist of his free hand. Cool Whip–white spittle formed in the corners of his mouth as he screamed, "Bitch, don't question me! Just do as I say and quit staring at their pricks."

Pete smiled and said, "Still carry that shit case like you gonna rob a bar, need to bind up a few fellas' wrists and ankles afterward? Like that couple we did a few back before you stole all Lang and me's shit?"

Ned pointed the pistol at Pete, said, "Don't know what you's talking about." Told Liz, "Go get the fucking tape."

Liz got the tape from the glove box. Began circling Elbow and Pete. Taping them to Dodge, who sat between them in his wheelchair. Liz striped them each from shoulder to waist, trying to decide when she'd ditch this backstabbing son of a bitch.

Ned squirted the honey all down their heads. Faces. Over the tape. Threw the empty bottle to the carpet.

Laughed, told them, "Gonna leave the door open when we leave. This is what I like to call a redneck flytrap."

Liz and Ned grabbed the bagged meth and coffee can of money, went out the door. Heard Pete hollering, "Gonna get yours fuckhead, gonna get yours!"

•

Jarhead reached for small trees. They uprooted and he kept sliding. The decline was two or three hundred yards straight down. He rolled and tumbled but held on to the Walmart sack. He hit bottom and lay on his back, cut and bruised, catching his wind. Dried leaves down his shirt and pants. Soil about his hands and knees.

From back up the hill, he could hear the faint crack and pop of gunfire echoing.

Making it to his feet, wiping away the debris of nature, he heard water splashing in front of him. He inhaled, followed the scent and sound. His boots sank into the marsh-mallowed earth. Vegetation had been drowned out. Trees were all that remained, their bare roots above land.

As he stepped out of the woods, there it was—the warm fish-stink of the Ohio River, its brown water beating the shoreline of mud and silt. Then like the wind a man's voice asked, "Shit happen to you, son? Get into a scrape with a sticker bush or was it Alonzo Conway?"

Back up the hill in the farmhouse, Alonzo aimed for the rear end of a police cruiser while Tig aimed for another. Kept pulling the trigger. Replacing a spent shell with a live one in succession. Till the plan took.

One ball of flame created another ball of flame. Bodies behind the cruisers disintegrated. The orange ball mushroomed wide and into the tin-sided barn, where flame found more fuel. Building into a large combustion. Shaking land and homes for miles.

Down on the Ohio, Jarhead and the man felt the tremor in their wobbling legs. Each glanced up the hill. "Sam hell was that?" the man asked.

Jarhead held a straight face of nicks and cuts. Tiny rips lined the weighted-down Walmart sack in his left hand. The .45 was tucked tight into his waistband. The man held a Quantum fishing rod in his right hand. Wore a brown T-shirt. Had a curved skinning knife attached to a pair of tan Carhartt carpenter pants tucked into black rubber wading boots. He was clean-shaven, his hair overcast-gray and long, banded into a ragged ponytail. Each ear was pierced. He'd eagles inked about his wadded-paper-sack arms. His eyes were bright green. Jarhead asked him, "You get me to the other side of the river?"

The man smiled, said, "Thought you'd never ask. Been waiting down here all morning."

Jarhead said, "Waiting all morning? Look, old-timer, cut the shit. Can you get me across the river and to Orange County or not? I gotta—"

"I know."

Sweat coated the ache that began to form on Jarhead's body. He was losing patience, started to pull the pistol from his waist and asked, "Whaddaya you mean you know? You in hock with them two diaper-raping motherfuckers up over the hill?"

The man's hand pressed against Jarhead's, stopped him from pulling the gun, and the man told Jarhead, "None of the above, son. I's strictly of the spirit. Now, put your ego back up. My boat's down behind you a few." He turned his hand into a handshake. "Name's Purcell."

Jarhead gripped Purcell's hand. "People call me Jar—"

"Jarhead Johnny Earl." Purcell squeezed his hand, said, "I know all about you. People call me Purcell, Purcell the Prophet sometimes. Let's get going 'fore it gets dark."

14

Cigarette smoke thick as the smoke from blazing tires wrapped around Angus at the door. Behind him, a rusted-exhaust-pipe voice laced with bourbon demanded, "Where you think you're going?"

Angus's mouth was devoid of moisture, dry as three Sundays without a drop of rain. He'd no pain. Just petrol in search of a spark. He fished a smoke from the pocket of his sleeveless gray T-shirt, lit it, and exhaled. "Fixing to get a drink chased with some answers."

A man. Midforties. Black T-shirt wrinkled around the collar. Chicken-skin flesh. Jaws rough lumps of biscuits browned in the oven too long. With a sixteen-penny-nail stare driving into Angus, he told him, "You're wrong. Ruined my boy with that shit you sell."

From the jukebox, Bascom Lamar Lunsford wailed "I Wish I Was a Mole in the Ground." A few men sat at a table behind the man, shaking their heads and sipping sweaty cans of Falls City. Angus let the cigarette dangle from his lip. His arms hung loose at his sides like an ape's. He took in the man's worn appearance, said, "You wanna bruise me up? Meet me outside when I'm done. But here's a warning, you're good as ash scattered in fresh loam when I finish with you."

The man's frame pulsed tight. "Why, why you gotta intrude here?"

Angus steadied himself, clenched a fist. Got the blood flowing, said, " 'Cause I gotta find someone to earn my keep. Every man makes a living off another human being, that's life."

The man dribbled, "You mean ruin people. Cause them impurities of life."

Angus inhaled deep. Drew the smoke into his lungs, blew it from his mouth while telling the man, "I get by on what's been dealt to me."

•

The man wouldn't quit, said, "That ain't God's way."

Angus laughed. Couldn't help it. "And getting shit-faced in a tavern is? Look, if they's a God, I'm doing right by his examples set upon man, woman, and child. Guess you are too."

The man clenched his teeth. "Don't say that."

Angus had had his fill, said, "Whatever your damage is with me, take it outside to the shit-green Pinto. Be there in a few."

Angus brushed the man's shoulder. Felt the give, the unbalanced push of his frame. Inexperienced, Angus thought, knowing he'd take the bastard out in two licks.

He made his way through the noise of bodies. Late

evening slurps. Hoots and howls. Sat at the bar. Poe met him with a slow push of words. "Ain't seen you in a long while. Your girl was in here few nights back."

Angus didn't even smile, said, "Why I'm here."

Poe told him, "You's a few nights shy, friend."

Unblinking, Angus ripped Poe's eyes out with his own, said, "You ain't my friend. But you can be friendly."

Poe held the dead gaze of the pearl eye in Angus's face and asked, "How's that?"

"We can do this civil. Or I can dislocate your shoulder. Segregate your eyes. Then drag your ass over this bar. Make things real bad for you in the coming years. I need to know where the girl, *my sister*, went with a fella named Ned."

Poe, cadaver-faced, channeled the noise of patrons in and out. The smell of smoke and booze lacquered his frame. The jukebox stopped. His heart rushed. A new song was coming. He took in Angus's shoulder with the white bandage. Thought about digging it open with the fork that lay below his crotch behind the bar. Angus interrupted, "Don't think that wound will slow me down none regardless of what you try. Just spit it to me straight. I'm out of your hair. No foul."

"3 Dimes Down" by the Drive-By Truckers started on the jukebox. Guitars whined: *It was a straight shot. All it took was luck to not get caught. I laid three dimes down and the machine wanted twenty-five cents.*

Poe knew Ned and this Liz were in the middle of something bad. Couldn't be good. Poe knew Ned always burned his bridges. And Poe'd heard about Angus. Never lost a fight. That was the rumor. Apparently the dumb shit at the door hadn't heard that one. Either way, it didn't matter. If Poe told Angus what he wanted, Ned might be pissing blood by morning if it weren't for several others wanting to make him do the same. Angus wouldn't find Ned before the others found him. But Lang and the others might be willing to trade their prize for some cash. Then again, that'd be between them and Angus. Like he said, no foul.

Poe told him, "You ever hear of a place called Cur's Watering Hole?"

Angus nodded.

Poe grinned. "How about the Donnybrook?"

•

Behind dark-tinted windows, Fu sat in a dusty navy blue Tahoe. He'd been staking out the tavern. Entrance in the front. Exit out the side. Was waiting till after midnight. Let the crowd get good and wobbled before he found the man named Poe. Didn't need every backwoods brother, cousin, and father getting fiery with him if he had to bloody the man.

Fu watched a man exit the tavern as quick as he'd entered. Lean barbed-wire muscle beneath sleeveless cotton. Tattoos in gothic script and a braided cord of hair down his back. Another man exited after him, stood by a rusted car. Near the same age. Waited. Feet unsteady. No balance. Carried himself all wrong. Started to approach the man dressed in the T-shirt without sleeves. Whose left hand came like a blink. Raised from his side. Separated the night. Met the man who waited by the rusted car. Made his nose plywood-flat. Rocked his head back. Clenched his jaw, which cracked along with his teeth. Blood smeared the air. The rocking wasn't from the left hand. The left hand hid the right uppercut that followed from the twist and dig of the right hip. The man who waited by the car fell to the gravel lot. The man who dropped him helped him to his feet. Escorted him back to the tavern's entrance.

Fu glanced at the photos that sat on his dash. This was the man with the puzzle-pieced face. He could fight. Held a form of honor. But there was no woman. Fu didn't need unwanted attention. Needed to question the man in solitude. Get Mr. Zhong's money. Fu opened his glove box. Pulled out plastic twist ties. Popped the back door open. Clicked the interior dome light off. Opened his door.

Angus heard the distant squeak of a car door. Faint crunches across gravel. Felt a presence flare in his neck. He released his car door's handle. Turned with his gun removed from his waistband. Raised it too late. Someone hit a nerve in Angus's arm. It went limp. He released the gun. The same quick hand caught it. A fist straight-lined him, the index finger bent, thumb on top of it, caught him below his nose. Delivered a loss of motor function throughout his body.

Angus fell forward. Was broken at the waist over a small man's shoulder. Carried and thrown facedown into the rear of a vehicle that smelled like leather seats and noodles with beef. Angus's elbows were twisted and bent behind his back. The wound in his shoulder burned. Wrist laid over wrist. Then tightened. He couldn't move them. A cloth sack slid over his head. The door slammed. The engine started.

Soon Angus sat with his head spinning. Cloth sack over

his head. He'd been pulled from the back of the vehicle. Carried from the outdoor heat to the indoor cool of AC. His hands were still pulled behind him. Restrained. His back pressed into the cold wood of a chair. Wherever he was smelt of fresh-poured concrete. Basement, maybe. Footsteps were light. Near silent. He started to move when he felt the pierce of metal. Something needle-fine passed through his flesh, hit a nerve. His legs went limp. He felt another pierce of metal. His arms lost feeling. *Fuck!*

The sack was removed from his head. Overhead lights burned bright. Angus sized up the small man. Saw flat-knuckled hands attached to arms bone-hard. The man wore glasses, his eyes snakelike behind the deep lenses. He stood by a small jade table. A stainless steel dish sat on top of it. Long needles lay inside it. The smell of rubbing alcohol.

Behind the man, two large leather sacks were suspended from the rafters by chains. Stuffed like punching bags. Shoulder level. Angus started to open his mouth, was cut off by the Asian man's tongue.

"My name is Fu. I work for a man named Mr. Zhong. He has a client, Mr. Eldon, who owes a large gambling debt. Mr. Zhong tells me you and your sister have an agreement for the exchange of money to Mr. Eldon. Money that he needed to pay Mr. Zhong. As it now stands, Eldon is dead. So you and your sister must pay the said money to Mr. Zhong to make all parties involved happy."

All Angus wanted was to find Liz and Ned, get his dope. Any money they had, he wasn't sharing. But sitting here paralyzed with a needle in his neck wasn't helping. He'd try his luck with the slant. "I don't got your money. My sister and some swinging cock took all that pervert Eldon's cash. And the drugs. Left me for dead. How I got the new shoulder decoration."

Fu didn't blink. "Why were you at the bar?"

Angus said, "Same as you. Looking for my sister and some guy goes by the name Ned. She hung out there. Sold our crank from time to time."

Fu questioned, "Why did you have a feud with the man in the lot?"

Angus chuckled. "Misunderstanding." He wanted to deal, laid a few cards on the table. "But I know where my sister's headed."

Fu's face lightened from stone to violently sweet powdered sugar. "Where?"

Angus said, "Look, you pull these needles out of me, untie my hands, we can talk."

Fu shook his head. "You tell me," he lied, "then I'll let you go."

Angus clenched his teeth. Tried another set of cards, said, "You can have the money. I want my crank. Wanna watch Liz and this Ned guy swim in they own filth. Look, I ride shotgun, give directions while you drive."

Fu stood, considering. Remembered Angus leading the man he'd dropped with two punches back to the bar. The way he'd carried himself. He'd some hint of reverence. Fu asked, "So, you will tell me where to drive? And we will get the money from your sister?"

Angus said, "Yeah, they's a ways off the beaten path. No offense, I tell you where they is, you get lost in the sticks, the sticks people ain't none too fond of giving your kind directions."

Fu considered this. Didn't need trouble. If he killed

Angus now, Mr. Zhong might have to wait even longer than he already had. Mr. Zhong was twenty grand in the hole from Eldon. Wanted his money now. Fu nodded. Stepped to Angus. A grunt erupted from one of the suspended leather bags. Fu stopped and turned in one motion and said, "Quiet!"

His voice bounced in the concrete room. The grunt turned to panting. The leather bag started to flail and expand violently. Angus's eyes bugged. His heart sped up. Fu approached the bag. Quick as the wind, he struck the bag with a right palm. A left elbow. The bag bent and jerked. The noise ceased. A spot formed on the bottom. Darkened the leather. Began to drip onto the gray tiled floor along with the faint sound of crying.

Fu laughed, explained to Angus, "Students."

He grabbed another needle from the dish. Calm as a clear blue sky. Stepped toward Angus and slid behind him. Angus tried to tense his body but was devoid of feeling.

Fu thought about the obsidian butterfly knife in his pocket. Glanced at the braided scalp of Angus. Imagined the blade parting Angus's throat halfway. Methodical and slow. Taking away his air. Watching the blood bubble and seep. Watching Angus cough, fight for air.

Angus tried to jerk and asked, "Motherfucker, we got a deal?"

Fu smiled. Pushed the needle into the side of Angus's neck. He went lights out. Fu whispered, "We have a deal. But now, you sleep."

•

Purcell lit a Marlboro Red. Smoke trailed from his mouth along with words. "Refresh me on why you's running from Alonzo Conway's property." He waved his fingers in the air. "It's a bit muddled."

Jarhead drummed his fingers on the hardwood table. Cuts on his face cleaned. His body scented with Irish Spring. Purcell had offered him to stay overnight. Get some food and rest. Said he'd drive him to Orange County in the morning. Jarhead explained, "Broke down outside of Frankfort. Tig give me a ride. Said he'd get me to Orange County. Helped him siphon some gas along the way. Didn't really know what-all he and his cousin Alonzo was into. He offered me a teenage girl for sex. He wanted to pay me for helping him and Tig out. Didn't want no part of it. That's when the police showed up. So I got out of there. How you know Alonzo?"

Purcell smirked. "Know everyone on both sides of the Ohio River. Know what they do. Who they fornicate with. When they shit. Alonzo and Tig is into anything that brings cash. Whores and guns, mainly. Also know you ain't from around here."

Jarhead nodded. "From Hazard, Kentucky."

Purcell shook his head. "I know. It's pretty country."

Jarhead said with sarcasm, "Right, you know everything. Like how Hazard's real pretty, but they's no jobs. Can't even get your foot in at the coal mines like my stepfather did."

Purcell flipped his ash into the ashtray. "They's no jobs anywhere these days. Gonna keep being fewer and fewer."

Jarhead said, "Seems the only way a man can make a

living without going to school anymore is to get his hands dirty, run some kind of illegal trade."

Purcell said, "World's changed. Time is come when education, self-improvement don't matter. It's come back to a man's got to know what he's good at. Your history will either help or hinder."

Jarhead waved the smoke from his face and said, "History?"

Purcell said, "Your kin. What they done did hoping to make this world a better place. Things your father and grandfather learned you. How to use your hands. Plant a garden. Hunt. Fish. Fight. What some seem to forget is history is now doomed to repeat itself, seeing as ain't nobody learned from their mistakes. Now no one can stop what has started."

Lost, Jarhead asked, "What's started?"

Purcell told him, "We're at the beginning of a violent era. Jobs are gone. Self worth and moral values have been sold. Some, like Alonzo, even prey on children. Film it, take pictures of it, and sell it. They's too much freedom, addiction, fear, and violence blinding us from the truth."

Jarhead crossed his arms across his chest, convinced that Purcell was fifty-two cards shy of a full deck, and asked, "What truth?"

Purcell could read Jarhead's expression, his thoughts. "That things have fallen apart. Everything our kin suffered to build is being disassembled. Criminals run everything now, government, everything. Gangsters the only one seeing any profit. We got no jobs, no money, no power, no nothin', nothin' to live for 'cept vice and indulgence. That's how they control us. But it's falling apart. What we got is our land and our machines, our families, and our ability to protect it all, to keep them alive. We got our hands. Ones who'll survive will be the ones can live from the land. Can wield a gun. Those folks'll fight for what little they've got. They'll surprise the criminals with their own savagery. Man, woman, and child will be tested. Others'll be too weak and scared. Uneducated in common sense. Won't know what's happened. But believe me, war is coming."

Jarhead sat lost in thought. Finally asked, "You expect me to believe this?"

"Why you think I was waiting for you? Did you see any fish in my boat? How you think I knew your name, where you was headed? You got a girlfriend named Tammy Charles, two mouths to feed with her. One named Caleb, the other named Zeek. You robbed a man in Hazard of one thousand dollars. Not a dollar more, not a dollar less. You plan on paying him back. Your girl Tammy is pained from a family member that you rescued her from. She's addicted to—"

"Stop!" Jarhead shouted, raised his hands, palms facing Purcell, unable to swallow this prophet's pill. He said, "Fine, say I believe you. How the hell would you know any of this?"

Purcell stubbed out his smoke, said, "Things come to me I can't explain. Names. Faces. They actions. I see them. Have to put them in place. Sometimes it's too late. Other times it ain't. All I know is you need to get to Orange County. I need to get you there. So's you can fight in the Donnybrook. It's your calling. Our calling."

"Calling? For what?" Jarhead asked.

"That part ain't come to me yet."

15

Kildrett and May Farnsley were shit-heel kin to Govern Farnsley. Living on his property. Producing children like mice in a cage. Cooking meth. Selling it. Snorting it. Smoking it. They weren't the ones killed Eldon, the ones Whalen was searching for. They, like Officer Meadows, lay in the Harrison County Hospital. Meadows with third-degree chemical burns about his face and arms. The Farnsleys with gunshot wounds. The kids with Child Services.

Sheriff Moon Flispart, newly elected, was pissed off. Wanted to know what Deputy Sheriff Whalen thought he was doing, searching abandoned houses down in bum-fuck. Whalen hollered while the nurse bandaged his left leg in the ER. "Thought I's searching for some meth-cook killers."

Moon bitched, "Got two gunshot victims, Child Services up my ass like two dozen hemorrhoids ready to burst for three children being raised like animals and maced, and an officer laid up 'cause of your horseshit Dirty Harry way of handling things."

Whalen yelled, "It was probable cause. They's cooking meth. I smelt it."

Moon hollered, "Here's my probable cause. I'm taking your badge till further investigation. You'll be having a hearing at the Sellersburg State Police Post in forty-eight hours."

That'd been over twelve hours ago. The sun had brought on a new day. Three hours of sleep. Pot of coffee. Shit and shower. Whalen pulled on a black T-shirt, worn-out Levi's. Laced up his work boots. Grabbed his 9-mm Glock for personal protection, seeing as Sheriff Moon had taken his service Glock. Fuck him. He'd find these bastards. Knew where he'd start. Part of being a county cop in a small town—Whalen knew where everyone laid their heads to rest. He'd do this the old-fashioned way.

•

Logs had started to moss over. Matched the tin roof's shade, hunter green. The Blue River ran just as green on the other side of the road. That hint of fish smell wafted into Whalen's inhale. The yard was littered with beer cans and pine needles. A small brown fridge sat on the wooden deck up next to the cabin's front door.

Whalen opened the fridge. Pulled a matching bottle from it. No name for this brew. Poe's personal batch. Whalen smirked. Pushed the bottle up into the flaking silver bottle cap opener attached to the side of the cabin. Popped it open. Swigged near the entire contents. His eyes peeled tears at the cold. He stepped to the front door. His fist met the gray hardwood. He raised the bottle again. Finished it. Listened to the steps behind the door. Locks clicking. Tarnished knob turning.

Poe's Colonel Sanders skin was wrinkled. One sleep-crusted eye was open, one closed. His pasty lips rattled, "Ross?"

Whalen brought the empty bottle down. Exploded it over Poe's forehead. Pulled him out of the doorway, onto the wooden deck. Bare feet over broken glass. Whalen gripped and twisted one of Poe's arms behind his back. Pressed his throat down over the wooden deck rail. Kicked his bare, boxer-short legs apart, taking Poe's movement from him.

Whalen said, "Gonna ask this one more time, Poe. What do you know about the people ran with Flat and Beatle?"

Slobbering awake, Poe arched his neck, tried to look up. Blood crowned his head and ran down into his eyes. He opened his parched lips and said, "A woman. Name's Liz. And her brother, name's Angus. He's scarred up on one side of his face. Long hair, wears it in a braid, like a Indian. Names and vines tattooed all up on his body. Liz got a build made of sin, hair all matted into clumps. She run off with Ned."

Whalen yelled, "That jack-o'-lanterned, fist-swapping fuck?"

Poe said, "Yeah, Ned. Liz come in the other night. They hooked up. She made a deal with Ned. Kill Angus, split his crank. Head down to the Donnybrook. Angus is headed that way too, looking for blood."

Whalen repeated, confused, "Looking for blood? Angus?"

Poe said, "He ain't dead. Ain't the dyin' type. He's alive and pissed off. Come in the bar the other night asking about Ned and Liz."

Whalen was shaking with anger. "Motherfucker!" He released Poe. "Always liked you. River-rat bar-back bastard! Caused a helluva mess. Put my badge on the line."

Poe rubbed his head and belched, "Why you have to bust that bottle over my damn head?"

Whalen yelled, " 'Cause I needed answers! Something I didn't get last time!"

●

Fu dialed Mr. Zhong on his cell while navigating the back roads of Orange County, the signal fading as he drove. Angus rode shotgun, hands twist-tied behind him, nodding directions when needed.

From the cell phone, Mr. Zhong asked Fu if he'd found the man and woman.

Fu told him he'd found the man.

Mr. Zhong wanted to know about the money. Fu told him he hadn't gotten the money, but he and the man were going to find the girl. That she'd left the man for dead and taken the money. Before the cell signal faded completely, Mr. Zhong asked where the girl was and Fu told him something called the Donnybrook.

He closed his cell phone. Placed it in his shirt pocket.

Beside him, Angus sat stiff from sleeping in the wooden chair. He broke the hushed AC hum. "Your boss?"

"You could say that. It's the man I am loyal to, yes."

The cold air clawed Angus's face. His bound arms goose-bumped as he watched the road. Wondered how much of the meth Liz and Ned had snorted. How much they'd sold.

Wondered what the shit Fu had hanging in them leather bags. Wasn't about to give Fu a chance to show him. Angus knew out here on the back roads of Orange County, even with his hands tied, he'd an edge. The slant was on his own, a hound without a scent.

Angus needed to free his hands. Knuckle his left fist into the slant's temple. Then put his right fist behind it. Pound his face into mushy skin and bone.

Fu pulled a smoke from his other breast pocket. Pushed in the lighter on the dash. The lighter popped out. Fu lit his cigarette. Inhaled an orange bur on its end. Smoke trailed from his lips as he spoke. "What you did to that man in the parking lot, he was blind to. Most American fighters, their movements are easy to read. Unless they have been trained by an Asian."

Angus saw his opening. "I's trained by my father. He's no Asian. But he boxed when he was in the army. Trained with a Thai boxer in Thailand. Filipino arts in the Philippines."

Fu pulled on the cigarette. "Your father understands discipline of training. Where the power of a strike originates. But also pressure point attacks. Your father, he knows honor in combat. Taught it to you very well."

Behind his back, Angus clenched and unclenched his fist. Open, closed. Open, closed. Thought of a time when all seemed balanced. Said, "He was an honorable man. Till I dishonored him."

Fu grinned, asked, "How so?"

Nodding to a stop sign in the distance, Angus pushed forward a bit. Created slack within the seat belt. Space between himself and the seat. Timed Fu's movements in his peripheral. "Hang a right at the stop. Follow the road about ten miles back." He paused. Asked, "Think you can light me one of them cancer sticks?" Fu hesitated, then nodded. Let his smoke hang from his lips. Fished out another. Lit it off his own. Laid it on Angus's lips without looking. Angus pulled on it. Mushroom clouds of smoke rounded from his mouth.

"Father taught me how to fight soon as I could stand. Banana punching bag in the barn. Speedball. No gloves, so I'd condition my hands. Mirror for hand-weighted shadow boxing. Rope for rhythm. He had his own logging business. Small operation. Made a good living. Taught the trade to me. Let me run it. Retired. I used to fight other loggers for money after work. Passed the time. Till I had me an accident with a saw. Kicked back into my face. No insurance. Found an under-the-counter plastic surgeon who butchered my appearance worse than it already was. I fell into a kind of darkness. Economy crapped out, lumber and building stalled. Sister got me hooked on meth. Perked me up. But it was too late. I lost the business. Started cooking the shit to sell for a living."

Fu interrupted, "And this is how you met Mr. Eldon."

Angus said, "Right, how I met Eldon. And that's how I disgraced my father."

Fu said, "Most Americans do not have any discipline. My country is all about discipline. Here in the United States, it is all about choice. You made the wrong one."

Angus bit down on the smoke, turned to Fu, and lunged forward, guiding the orange marbled glow into the flesh of

Fu's right cheek. Cigarette tobacco and ash erupted. Tires barked. Fu jerked, kept one hand on the wheel. Angus twisted his upper body and shoulders up out of the seat, drove the side of his head into Fu's head. Over and over. Knocked Fu's head into the driver's side window. Fu tried to palm him away. Angus fell back. The seat belt caught. Jerked. His neck gave. His head met the passenger's side window. He dug down into the side of the seat, found where the seat belt locked. Worked and fumbled with the button to unlock the belt. The Tahoe slowed down, ran off the side of the road. The seat belt released.

The car sat idling, half off the road, next to a barbed-wire fence that enclosed a pasture of old hay. Angus pushed his back into the passenger door. Pulled his knees to his chest. Drove his boots into the side of Fu's head. Busted it through the driver's side window. Glass rainbowed out the door. Blood poured from Fu's head. Angus kicked him again. Took in where the lighter was located. Turned his back to the console. Pushed against it. His fingers found the lighter. Pushed it in.

Fu's eyelids fluttered. Blood ran from his nose, mouth, a gash on the left side of his skull. His glasses hung down his nose, right and left sides cracked.

The lighter popped. Angus fingered it out. Bent his wrist, turning the heated end into the plastic twist ties that bound him. Singed skin and plastic. Smelt the burn. Felt his hands free.

Fu shook his head. Turned to Angus, dazed. Angus loaded Fu's vision with knuckles. Reached across him. Opened the driver's side door. Pushed him out. Fu hit the heated grass flat on his face, tried to crawl away, get his senses. Angus stepped out, stiff. Walked to Fu, bent down. Punched him in the back of the head. Pressed a knee into his spine, took Fu's wallet. Old habits die hard.

Angus turned back to the idling Tahoe. Pulled a wad of bills from the wallet. Pushed them into his front pocket. Dropped the wallet. Felt pain pelt his right kidney. Then his spine. Dropped to his knee. Felt hands reaching for his head of hair. Turned left and right-hooked Fu's left inner thigh. Shot a left uppercut into his crotch. Fu backpedaled. Angus stood up, met a left elbow. Right knee. Took it, felt the slice of blood across his skull. Returned a blur of jabs and hooks with Fu deflecting them on his arms. Angus kicked low. His shin met Fu's. He threw a cross that softened Fu's face. Knocked him backward. Made his body twitch and convulse.

Angus stepped back, panting, his hands raised. Winded. Gunshot wound aching.

He started to laugh. Fu had fallen into a barbed-wire fence and gotten tangled. His every movement made the barbs cut deeper into his flesh.

Angus limped to the idling truck. Got in. Put it into drive.

•

Whalen had less than thirty-six hours before his hearing in Sellersburg. Less than thirty-six hours to find this Angus and Liz. But he'd neglected the farm. He needed to check on his nephew, as he did every couple weeks.

He took a detour down the valley road, recollecting the call that had come over the radio that day nearly five years ago. First to arrive on the scene, seeing the old Ford in the distance, frayed outline in the road. He'd rushed from his vehicle. Found Doddy, her beauty splintered and spilled about the pavement. Skull scattered. Flies buzzing in the heat. The unborn hump inside of her, dead or suffocating. Ten feet from her sat the still-warm Ford. What was left of Reese dotted over the driver's side fender. Up across the hood. Barrel of his 16-gauge rested on his shoulder. Hands crimped about the trigger and stock.

His brother-in-law Reese had shot Doddy, then himself, because the truth was too much.

Now Whalen pulled down the weeded drive to the farmhouse left to him in the will along with the five hundred acres it sat upon. He parked his Jeep. Got out. The warm country air carried something rancid. Whalen walked up toward the house, like he had that day. Taking in the apple tree where his sister, Azell, and her daughter Tate sat slumped. Arms above their heads. Nailed into the old tree trunk, crucified for his sacrifice. What was left of their beauty matched the hue of ripe apple rind. Same as Doddy and Reese, features removed by 16-gauge slugs.

Whalen stood on the rock surface, his back to the house, knowing that no one else knew why Reese had gone mad that day. No one knew about Whalen's conversation with the man the previous night. The can of kraut he'd opened by confronting Reese because he was tired of watching his own grow up from a distance. A conversation that had killed the entire family. All except the boy, Gravel.

Gravel had made the call. Ross had found him in the one place he always hid, a cave up by the barn. Face swelled wet. Two of his digits gone. The boy explained best he could. Finding Reese in the kitchen after he'd been squirrel hunting. Reese standing over the kitchen sink. Madness in his eyes. The screams coming from the bathroom. Gravel finding his mother and sisters bound. Reese attacking him from behind. Beating him unconscious. Gravel playing possum when he awoke. Waiting till the house was silent. Calling 911. Running from the house. Hiding in the cave.

Whalen had kept the boy that way all these years. Letting the local law and people of Harrison County believe Gravel was dead. Buried somewhere unknown by Reese. It's what he and Gravel wanted. To be left alone. To forget that day. Their little secret.

Now, Whalen started to walk toward the barn, noticed the wash tub of water. The weeds that had been leveled by the sickle that leaned against the apple tree. The generator on the other side of the house. Extension cords roped from it to the farmhouse. He glanced at the door, open behind the screen. Removed his pistol from his waist, knowing Gravel rarely went into the house. Whalen opened the screen door, raised his tone. "Gravel?"

Inside the kitchen, windows were blacked over by spray paint and duct-taped garbage bags. The table was littered with household chemicals. Baggies, hot plates, mason jars. Gas lanterns on the counter. There was the scent of burning fused with coagulated blood. Chemical rot.

Glancing down at the floor, he took in the insects trailing the body. Whalen's Gravel.

Whalen kneeled down next to the boy, his fingertips brushing leaflets of hair. Bone-cold cheek. Dead. He'd been that way for a while. Bullet holes lined his chest. A 9-mm brass lay on the worn linoleum. Whalen inhaled. Bit his lip. His bloodline ended here, but he kept it together.

Standing up, he took in the distorted details. Someone had squatted in the house. Been cooking meth. In the sink lay three rabbits, their hides skinned. As though Gravel had been preparing them for someone. Still holding his gun, Whalen searched the rest of the house. In the back bedroom, he found a sleeping bag. No clothing. But a wallet lay on the floor. He opened it up. Could hardly believe the name on the license inside.

•

Two acne-scarred men in body-stained short sleeves sat at an upturned wire-spool table next to the entrance, hunting knives sheathed on their sides. Mason jars sweated in front of them. Angus walked through the door, his head and gunshot wound pulsing in unison. He followed the hum of ceiling fans past the empty tables to the bar on his right. Where two more men sat to his left sipping shots of bourbon, cigarette smoke forming the air around them. Each wore a yellow shirt. Across the backs, black lettering scribed the tavern's name: CUR'S WATERING HOLE.

The bartender turned around, towel tossed over his shoulder. Handlebar mustache, shade of tanned hide. Matching hair slicked back. Knuckle-sized holes in each ear. He pushed his hands onto the bar, nodded. "What'll it be?"

Angus felt everyone's eyes branding his flesh. "Poe sent me. Said to ask for a man named Lang."

The bartender looked to his right, nodded at the two men to Angus's left. Then over Angus's shoulder at the door where the two acne-scarred men sat. His eyes came back to Angus, and he said, "He called. Must be Angus."

Barstools and chairs screeched like a loose belt on a car's engine. The men to Angus's left stood up. Shadows poked Angus's peripheral. He gritted without hesitation, "Poe said you could point me in the direction of a man goes by Ned. Running with a female named Liz. Said they's headed to the Donnybrook."

Lang chuckled. "I know where they at. But it'll cost you."

Visions of a dog being thrown into a wood chipper that spit out every shade of red turned Angus's gut. He felt the two men from the table by the door break the ceiling fan's air behind him. Slow, cautious steps approaching. He wrinkled his eyes, asked, "Cost me? Sons a bitches left me for dead. Took off with my crank. I'd say they's already cost me plenty."

Lang nodded to the men on Angus's left, said, "You want them, gonna have to get in line with all the people Ned done bent over the wash basin. And tickets for the line ain't free. You'll be payin' me."

Angus glanced to his left. Outlines covered his view. He reached into his pocket with his right. Took in the thick glass ashtray of crunched cigarette butts on the bar to his left. Barstool in front of him. Pulled out a wad. Lifted it up. Held it for Lang to grab. Counted the two men's slow steps from the door as they smothered in from behind.

Lang said, "Now you're talking my language. I'll take that." Reached for the money. Angus dropped it on the bar. Lang leaned forward. Quick as a finger pulls a gun's trigger, Angus sent his right elbow across Lang's face. His left hand swiped the ashtray. He brought it across the other side of Lang's face, then knocked him back behind the bar with a right cross.

Angus hooked the barstool in front of him with his right foot. Lifted it up, grabbed it with both hands. Turned, threw it into one of the yellow-shirted men on his left. It tripped him and bent him forward. Angus stepped into him. Planted a right uppercut into his mouth. Spun around to the other yellow shirt, who'd circled to Angus's left and now cut the air with a stiff jab. Angus ducked his head. Jammed the man's punch with the top of his skull. Metacarpals and carpals shattered. The man gasped.

Angus drove a left hook into his jaw. Then a right hook to his kidney. Locked his arm, palmed, spun, and threw him into the two acne-scarred men from the door. Knocked them into a table.

From behind, Angus felt a boot heel knife his right calf muscle. Drive him down to one knee. Felt a fist knuckle the back of his skull. Angus raised his left arm to his head. Covered. Pivoted on his left foot. Turned his right fist into the man's groin. Doubled him forward. Fired a left elbow into the man's temple. Pushed to his feet and palmed the man's head up with him. Then dropped the man with a right cross.

Angus's lungs felt the frostbite of being winded. He turned, grabbed a barstool. Smashed it down into the other yellow-shirted man trying to get up behind him. Fought the huff that blocked his lungs.

The other acne-scarred man from the door got to his feet. Angus lined him with a jab to the face. Rocked his skull back. Closed his swallowing with a cross to the throat. The man's larynx shattered like porcelain. His hands grasped his throat for air that wouldn't enter, and he dropped to his knees.

The other man from the door brought a right cross. Nicked Angus's left cheek. Angus kicked him just below his navel. Took his center of gravity. Angus stepped to the man's side, drove five knuckles into the soft meat just below his armpit. Lung point. The man hugged himself and hit the floor.

Angus turned to the bar. Two-handed the surface, heaved himself over it. Felt his shoulder spotting with ache. Lang lay at the other end of the bar on his ass, hiding, blood about his nose and right eye and his left hand fumbling for the handle of a sawed-off double-barrel stuck into the bar above his head. He pulled it out. Thumbed back the triggers of both barrels. Angus's left arm followed his legs forward, raking the bottles of whiskey and vodka that sat lined up behind the bar down onto the floor as he heard the explosion of the sawed-off.

16

They circled and bumped one another like predators. Men with talcum teeth, skin cleaved by scars. Hair braided, slicked, or stringy. Short or shaved. Bearded or stubbled. Tall. Short. Lean, hard, or fat-bellied. They came in all demeanors. Donning bibs or jeans ragged as the boots laced around their feet. These were the backwoods bare-knuckle fighters.

Some punctured stolen canisters of freon. Dropped them into black plastic bags. Closed them up. Took turns meeting the openings with their faces. Huffing. Holding in the gas till the dizziness dented their perceptions, made surrounding voices echo, outlines wobble. Others snorted and shot meth. Felt the dopamine rush root through their minds like a bullet.

The circus of men spread out in front of the platform, waiting for a man to step up onto the graying wood and announce the first twenty numbers so the first of six free-for-all bare-knuckle fights could begin.

In the frays of field grass there were enough dented, dirty, and rusted vehicles to fill ten football fields, maybe more. From them, onlookers got out with lawn chairs and provisions. Set up camp. Their forest fires scented the air with smoke and the whole chickens or slabs of venison, goat, squirrel, rabbit, or coon they grilled. It's what they'd do for the next three days. Sell their food to others. Sit chasing pills and crank with swigs of bourbon or home brew. Watch twenty men enter a thirty-by-thirty barbed-wire ring, fight till one man was left standing. Then another twenty numbers were called for the next free-for-all. Till Sunday, when the winning men were left to fight till one man stood bloody and toothless waiting for his cash prize.

There was one way in, one way out, of the bare-knuckle festival: a gravel road, near a mile long, lined by pine trees on each side. A steel-slatted gate cut the road in half. Beside the gate was a tin-roof wooden shack painted black with gray trim. From inside stepped four men with long hair greased to their shoulders. Thick beards. Mirrored wraparound sunglasses covering their eyes. They dressed in faded T-shirts, aged denim, boots. Their flesh was tattooed with hearts—MOM knifing their centers—or MIGHTY MOUSE or WHITE PRIDE. Each man was armed with a shotgun. Tied outside the shack were two tan curs. Two brown-and-black Walkers. Two walnut bloodhounds.

The four men wanted to know if you were a fighter or an onlooker. They took your entrance fee if you were fighting, gave you a plastic number. Told you and your trainer to sleep in the horse stables up by Bellmont McGill's barn that overlooked the barbed ring. Separate from the onlookers, who paid one hundred bucks to watch, wager, camp, and sell food, booze, or drugs all weekend.

No one left till the fighting was finished. This was the rule of Mr. McGill. To cross him was to become part of the thousand acres of wild, unknown land he owned. To be seeded into the soil. Walked upon by the next group of men trying their luck the following year at Donnybrook.

After paying his fighter's fee at the entrance, Ned got his number. Liz would be an onlooker. They parked in the field lined and spread with trucks and cars, all makes and models. Saw men and women in their camps with raised bottles of booze. Their tents pitched. Fire pits blazing or grills smoldering. Voices humming like bees in a swarm. Liz sat rearranging herself, bitching, "Never let no man feel up my shit like they did."

Ned tongued a tooth the color of dry leaves, laughed. "You's far from being the Virgin Mary. I never seen 'em do that before no way."

"Look, Festus, you done give me enough surprises with them incest brothers. Didn't tell me we had to give these sons of bitches a thousand dollars to fight on top of one hundred so I could watch and sleep in a horse stable with you."

Ned got red-faced, said, "Can the lip, bitch. I done this more than a few. 'Sides, when I win this thing, won't matter no way. You just shake that shapely ass, jiggle them titties, and sell our meth."

Liz bit her tongue. Tasted blood. She was beyond pain. Tired of being called a female dog, of being told it was *their* meth. Tired of being an onlooker. She took a stab at his backwoods ego, told him, "How the shit some double-crossing drip-dick like you know about something like this?"

Offended, Ned told her, "Any man with two fists and something to prove knows about Bellmont McGill's Donnybrook. The coin alone separates the pugilists from the wannabes."

Ned opened the door to step out of the truck. Liz wondered why Angus had never fought in one of these Donnybrooks. Then she knew—he'd never part with no thousand bucks just to get in a fight. Too late now anyway. Sarcasm fed her laugh. She asked Ned, "You a wannabe or a limpdick pugilist?"

The truck door slammed with no reply. Liz thought, Fuck off. Opened her rucksack of meth. Dug Angus's pistol out of the bottom. Pushed it down the back of her hip-hugger jeans. Hefted the rucksack of meth. Opened the door. Stepped out to the smell of food on grills and smoke from fire pits. Ned came around the side of the truck, grabbed her arm. Slobber boiled in the corners of his mouth. "Look, you ain't nothing but a whore selling her flavors with a pinch of good crank. We finish here, we split our earnings, go our separates. Till then, get rid of the tangy tongue."

Liz looked into his mutted, uneven face. Thought about digging her teeth into his nose of oily blackheads. Chewing it off. Driving her knee up into his crotch. Dropping him. Spitting his mangled pieces back onto his face. Showing everyone Ned was a wannabe pus sack. She twitched her knee. Threw Ned off. He tightened his grip, spit, "Go 'head, bitch, see how quick I tame that rancid flavor you got brewing."

She jerked her arm from his grasp. Pumped her left knee up for effect. Ned dropped a hand, blocked her knee.

Leaned back, shook his head, showing his three teeth and gum smile. Liz's other hand reached behind her. Pulled, and then pushed Angus's pistol up under Ned's throat. "Hope you can read them fighters' movements better than mine or the only thing you'll be splitting is your insides."

Ned foamed, "Cunt."

Liz felt eyes from the surrounding onlookers as she pressed the barrel into his throat harder, told him, "I'm tired of talking with you. It's been nice. Now nice is over. Go try to do what you come to do. I'll do the same. See you in the stables."

She pulled the gun from his throat. Kept a bead on him. Backed away real slow. He stood rubbing the spot she poked into him, said, "Watch your ass, bitch. 'Cause I know I will." Then he took his thumb. Started on one side of his throat like it was a razor. Cut across to the other side. Spit on the ground. Turned with his plastic number in hand. Walked over to the crowd of fighters gathered around the large gray platform.

Behind Liz, a female voice said, "Don't pay Ned no mind. He's a backstabbing tool."

Liz turned around to see a faded blonde, her hair of jagged ends not passing her chin. She sat by a tent, drawing on a smoke, can of Bud sweating by her feet. A rusted-out green-and-white International Scout sat next to the tent. Her lips were pale as bleach. Eyes opaque. She wore a Lucero concert T-shirt. Cutoff desert fatigues. Brown and broken work boots. Held out a hand. "Name's Scar."

Liz approached. Got into her face. "Look, you crotch-nibbling bitch, I wanna mix with a backstabbing pugilist, it's my concern."

Scar swigged her Bud, smiled, not seeing the butt of Angus's gun coming down across the bridge of her nose. The Bud busted open on the ground. Scar's eyes watered. Her hands smothered her nose. She nasaled out, "Bitch!"

Liz finished with, "Ain't no dyke's concern no way."

•

Unable to decide whether Purcell was a batshit-crazy, chicken-shack recluse or a legit prophet like Da Mo, the curator of Shaolin Muscle-Tendon Changing Qigong, Jarhead distracted himself by watching the first twenty men trade knuckles, knees, and elbows. Pound one another's bones. Break and bruise skin. No matter how insane Purcell might be, at least he'd gotten him here.

He'd seen preachers with suitcases housing rattlesnakes. Pulling the snakes out during church services. Men, women, and children singing and dancing. Their eyes rolling white into the rears of their skulls. A snake being passed around to see if it bit them. Magicians, that's what his stepfather called them. Fools of their own apocalypse.

Purcell had given him a backpack for his clothing and pistol. Told him to keep the gun and the box of ammo buried beneath the clothing. That he'd be needing it. For what, Purcell wasn't sure yet.

He'd told Jarhead he'd stay with him for guidance.

Purcell kept studying the crowd of backwoods misfits. Jarhead asked, "Who you looking for?"

He smiled. "He ain't here yet, but the others are. Things are just gettin' started."

150

Jarhead asked, "Who ain't here yet? What things?"

Purcell smiled and said, "Watch. You'll see."

•

Blood blotted Whalen's hands like wood stain. Dried and cryptic, it highlighted the lines of his skin. Navigating his Jeep down the back road, he thought of how he'd thrown Gravel over his shoulder. Hauled him up beyond the barn into a small thicket of cedar. Taken a shovel from the milk house. Dug through limestone and red clay. Buried Gravel among his kin.

For five years, Whalen had checked on Gravel. Letting him live from the land in a cave that tunneled beneath the barn. Gravel had kept a garden. Made lye soap. Hunted his meat. Stored it in his makeshift fridge that sat in the earth. Boiled his water from the stream that ran through the bottom of the cave. Lived like a hermit. Just as Reese and Whalen had taught him.

Now this Angus or Liz who'd run with him—and murdered Beatle, Flat, and even Eldon—had killed his Gravel. There was no maybe. Whalen felt it suffocate his heart. This Angus and Liz were killers. Add Ned to the mix, and it looked as though Whalen would have his hands full. Regardless of his badge, when he found them he'd take them someplace and do as he pleased. Get the truth and bury it.

He hung a right at the stop sign. Knew he'd ten more miles to Cur's Watering Hole. Poe'd told him to ask for Lang. Lang would help him get to the Donnybrook, find this Angus who was after Liz and Ned.

151

Out his driver's-side peripheral, a figure rose up from the earth like the dead from their graves.

Whalen slammed on his brakes. Threw open the door. The heat of the day hugged his body with sweat. He stared at the purple and violet swells about the complexion of an Asian man. Who jerked one foot after the next toward the Jeep with his white shirt torn and bloody, dress slacks the same. He wore glasses with both lenses cracked. Cell phone in his hand.

Words fell from Whalen's mouth, a leaky faucet, saying, "The shit's a Chinese doing out in the damn sticks of Orange County?"

There was no soul nor sound for miles. Whalen took in the tears about the Asian's arms. Noticed the barbed-wire fence behind him. Son of a bitch must've fell into that, got tangled up. The man stood before him. His cheek pulsed a clear liquid from an opening the size of a cigarette's end. A burn, Whalen thought. And he raised his voice, asking, "The shit happen to you?"

The man looked at Whalen's shirt smeared a familiar shade from Gravel, told him, "A hitchhiker. He took my Tahoe."

Whalen thought, What a dumb son of a bitch. Got what you deserved. "Why the hell you out here in the sticks picking up hitchhikers?"

The man's flint-chipped face lit up seeing the gun on Whalen's hip. Whalen saw the reaction, raised a palm. The other hand touched the gun on his hip. He said, "I'm a county cop. It's okay." The man said nothing. Whalen asked again, "Why are you out here?"

The Asian said, "I'm taking care of some business."

Whalen's asshole tightened, him thinking, Business? And, seemed like someone had taken care of this guy's business, not the other way around. "What sort of business you got out here in the sticks?"

Fu didn't have time for Q and A. Wanted to move his hands, see how this cop with blood spatter about his torso reacted to his movements. See how he carried himself. Fu had let his guard down once. Almost cost him his life. But he thought, No fighting, he needed to get Mr. Zhong's money. Needed to calm himself. He fished a smoke from his shirt pocket and asked, "Do you know of a place called the Donnybrook?"

Whalen chuckled. "It's where I'm headed."

The unlit smoke hung from Fu's busted lip. "That is my business."

Whalen sized up the little Asian, asked, "You a fighter?"

Fu smiled at Whalen. "Sometimes I am."

Whalen held a soured cramp in his gut, said, "Get in if you want a ride."

Fu got in. Closed the door. Watched the man limp around the front of the Jeep. Open the passenger's side. Fall back into the seat and slam the door. Push his cell phone into his shirt pocket.

Whalen said, "Them cell phones don't take this far out in the sticks."

Fu nodded, saw the lighter. He pointed to it, asked, "May I?"

Whalen glanced at the lighter, said, "Sure." With his hand resting on his thigh, close to his gun, he thought, If the Asian tries anything, I'll blow the driver's side window out with the side of his head.

Fu pushed in the dashboard lighter. Kept a blurred peripheral on the gun attached to the cop's hip. The gun would be hard to pull from his side once the seat belt was fastened. Even now, with a blinding elbow, a quick index knuckle to the cop's lung point or kidney, he'd be left breathless. The gun was useless at in-fighting range. Fu asked, "Do you fight?"

Whalen thought of how he'd have to turn, pull his gun from the hip all at once. Push his back into the driver's side door, keep the spatter down. He wondered if this Asian was one of them karate-chopping sons of bitches. He knew that shit had its place. He'd seen *Billy Jack*. But no way a man could beat a bullet. He said, "No, just a peacekeeper."

"Peacekeeper," Fu repeated.

Fu sat in the seat, thought about how he'd kill this cop. But he needed him to get to the Donnybrook. Find Angus. His sister. Get Mr. Zhong's money. The lighter popped out. Fu grabbed it. Lit his cigarette. Pushed the lighter back in. Inhaled. Smoke traced his insides. Relaxed his mind. A smile blossomed from his lips as he imagined this cop pleading in his own blood.

•

Insects landed and stuck to soured flesh that'd been coated sweet. Pete and Elbow grunted and struggled to get loose, just as they had for hours. With the same outcome. Muscles stiffened with ache.

Out the open door, footsteps stumbled into the small house. Lang's voice barked, "What the shit?"

Pete hollered, "Lang!"

Lang entered the house with fresh abrasions. Ashtray to the temple, elbow-busted nose. Wrists belt-tied behind his back.

A boot heel kicked Lang to the carpet.

Angus held the sawed-off. Both barrels reloaded. Box of shells in the Tahoe. A few shot shells in his pants pocket. Lang had missed Angus by centimeters back at the bar. After the glass of busted booze bottles rained down on Lang, Angus had filled his vision with left and right square-dancing heel stomps. Now Angus stared at the men tied together. Pale. Bony. Mange-infested and exposed. He said, "Fuck sakes, what kind of queers you running with, Lang?"

Pete, bare feet and balls naked, whined, "Who the shit are you?"

Angus ignored Pete's words, pushed the sawed-off down into Lang's skull. "Where the shit's Ned and Liz with my crank? You said they'd be here getting corn-holed."

Lang motioned his dented head to Pete, Dodge, and Elbow. Spit blood, said, "Ask them."

Angus asked, "The shit you all got on yourselves, smells like honey?"

Dodge chattered his teeth like a copperhead shakes its tail. Pete started to cry, said, "It is. That faggot son of a bitch Ned and his peacock-headed bitch took Elbow's gun and Dodge's money. Made us all get naked. Duct-taped us together. Poured honey all over us. Bastard shot Dodge in his leg. Now, will you cut us loose?"

Angus said, "Let me guess, they're headed to the Donny-brook."

Pete blew air through his nostrils, a child pouting, said, "Yeah."

Dodge jerked his upper body back and forth. Hollered, "Cut us loose. Get these naked parasites off me. Want my Fruity Pebbles, a PBR, and my goddamn money back."

Pete's eyes welled with tears, him pleading, "Please, just cut us loose."

Dodge pushed his mouth to Pete's head, bit into his hair, growling and ripping it from the roots, tasting and spitting the honey and sweat. Pete screamed. Thrashed his head into Dodge's, who shouted, "Shut up, you pussy, shut up!"

Wanting out of this freak-show house hidden in the woods, Angus clutched Lang's hair, yanked him to his feet, said, "Come on, you're taking me to the Donnybrook. Now." Angus pushed Lang out the door. Behind him he heard the man in the wheelchair holler and spit, "Come back here, you fuckers, come back!"

17

Onlookers ingested teaspoon-scoops of crystal up flared nostrils. Ran it with swigs of booze and hollered, "Make 'em bleed!"

Jarhead wiped specks of parched saliva and blood from his forehead, measured the onslaught of men in the ring. Their stutter-steps of unsure footing. Punches thrown wild from the shoulder, not the hip. He thought they fought like starved hogs wallowing in the mud. Snorting and wheezing for air.

Jarhead clenched his left fist, whitened his knuckles for Caleb. Then his right for Zeek. He'd win, he told himself. Give his boys a better life. Get Tammy the help she needed. Fix her back. Cease the Oxycontin dependency. But would he quit fighting? Stop the one thing he was gifted at?

Behind him, a shoulder brushed his own. He turned, watched a female with serrated lengths of hair calculate her each and every step. A beer bottle held at her side like a blade. Bumping through the crowd of abuse.

Beside him, Purcell said, "You can't quit."

Jarhead turned to Purcell and said, "Quit what?"

Purcell said, "What you was just considering up yonder." Purcell tapped an index finger to his temple. Looked at the ring and asked, "Think they's any count?"

In the ring, three men hit the ground like squirrels shot from a tree. No bounce, just muscle and bone collapsing to a halt.

Jarhead wondered how much Purcell knew about his future as he turned back to the female. Watched her hone in on her prey. His heart rushed, and he said, "They footing and punches is off balance, unsure. Mostly they's scrappers at best."

Purcell turned around to where Jarhead was looking and asked, "Sam hell you keep gawking at that female for?"

Jarhead's frame tightened with adrenaline and he said, " 'Cause she's surefooted."

•

Liz walked among booze-breathed men who were sweat-sheened and pumped as they watched the first twenty men fight. She offered her godliness in clear baggies for one hundred and twenty-five to one hundred and fifty a dose. Offered it to the ones with missing teeth and dehydrated appearances first, knowing they'd an itch for it.

From close range, Scar watched. Dabbed her busted tomato nose, muttered to herself among the depravity of hooting and hollering male and female onlookers, "Someone's gonna spit and piss blood."

She sang it over and over like a lullaby.

Liz worked her way through salt-scented bodies,

stopping in front of the thirty-by-thirty square ring. Ned's number had been drawn. In the ring, he and nineteen other men taunted and faked with their heads and arms. Fisted, elbowed, kicked, stomped, palmed, kneed, and head-butted one another into paste. Specks of each misted out of the ring onto the shrieking onlookers.

Sunlight bit down on Ned. It'd already begun to lather his and the other fighters' frames, making punches slip and palms slap from their bodies. The loose rock they fought on uprooted their footing, kept them off balance.

Liz watched Wolf Cookie Mike plant the ball of his right foot and dig an uppercut into Ned's stomach. Roll off with a right hook to his ribs. Ned coughed. Dropped his forehead down onto Mike's face. Bone cracked. Red-hued his upper lip. Ned pumped a triple left jab. First to Mike's jaw. Then his throat and shoulder. Mike stepped back. Tried to shake it off. Ned followed with an elbow. Parted the soft skin above Mike's right eye.

Whistles and yelps amped up from the men and women watching.

"Beat that son of a bitch, Ned!" someone screamed.

"Come on, Wolf Cookie Mike! Kill that backstabber!" Someone else.

Liz worked a finger into the baggie of moist powder she kept for herself. Vacuum-inhaled. Tasted the chemical drain down her throat. Wiped her teeth with the remaining specks on her finger. Turned to a man in a clean white T-shirt tucked into jeans. Hair short. Split on one side. Coffee-bean brown with flecks of gray. Thorny complexion. Red, yellow, and orange flames sleeving each arm.

He smiled. She felt moisture glisten down below. Ned had been impressing her in the ring, she'd admit that. But this man had presence, something tougher than that greasy-haired dime bag dealer. She pointed to the ring and hollered over the cheers, "Why they call him Wolf Cookie Mike?"

The man laughed, grasped her arm, said, "I gave him that name." He nodded them away from the hollering, promising the rest of the story.

Scar squinted her eyes. Dropped the rag from her nose, kept the pair of them in her sights. Took a hard swig of Bud. "Someone's gonna spit and piss blood."

Liz and the man walked to where they could view the fight but speak without yelling. The man's lips parted, offered his deep southern Indiana dialect. "Years back, Mike's at Cur's Watering Hole after working a local sawmill. Stew Coats bumps into him. Accident. Mike spills his beer. Coats apologizes, offers to buy him another. Mike's got a buzz, threatens Coats. Says he's gonna beat him into a shade of afterbirth. Coats laughs, tells Mike to calm down. Mike don't calm down. Coats is six foot six. Two hundred fifty pounds. Gristled tobacco farmer. Mike, as you can see, five-six. Hundred sixty pounds. Mike keeps on. Starts digging his finger into Coats's chest. Mike tells him, 'Let's step out to the lot.' Coats nods okay. The whole tavern clears out to watch. Coats stands out in the graveled lot, face the shade of a rash. Mike says, 'Wait one second.' Walks over, opens his truck door. Pulls out an axe handle. Approaches Coats. Offers it to him, says, 'You gonna need this.' Whole tavern is watching. Coats stares at Mike for near a minute.

Then he says, 'You're fucking crazy.' Walks back into the tavern."

Scar snaked around men and women, keeping a bead on Liz.

Liz ignited her brain with another inhale of the moist powder, asked, "The hell Mike do that for?"

The man smiled, offered, "Ran into Mike on down the line. Ask him, 'The shit was you thinking that day you threatened Coats? He could've killed you.' Mike laughed, said, 'But he didn't. I sold that son of a bitch a mess of wolf cookies. He thought I's as crazy as I was stupid. He didn't know what to do.'"

Behind Liz, voices rose around the ring. Five men lay unmoving on the ground. Fifteen traded blows. Ned stomped Mike's face into a puddle of defeat. Went to another man. Double-teamed him with another fighter. The man fell. Ned traded with the man he'd helped.

Liz sniffed twice, offered her hand. "Can call me Liz."

Scar came up behind Liz. Empty beer bottle in hand. Nose shading to black and yellow. She raised the bottle. Shattered it over Liz's head of possum tails.

Surrounding mouths shouted, "You see a head, hit it! You see a head, hit it!" Over and over.

With an intense stare, the man watched Liz's form gel up and drop. He bent down, his hand lifting her chin. Said, "Name's Bellmont McGill. And this is my daughter, Scar. Welcome to the Donnybrook."

Scar pulled out the gun tucked down the rear of Liz's painted-on denim. Ripped the rucksack from her back. Liz tried to fight. Scar fed the butt of the pistol into Liz's mouth till she traded fighting for pink saliva. Scar slid the gun down the front of her fatigues. Opened the rucksack. Dug her hand down inside. Shouted, "Goddamn!"

•

Tables lay upturned. The insides of men redesigned the floor. Two outlines stood behind the bar of Cur's Watering Hole, their faces welted and busted. The shelf behind them sat devoid of liquor. One man shouted, "The shit you want?"

The smell of combined bourbons pried Whalen's inhale and he said, "Looking for Lang. Poe sent me."

Uneasy laughter hummed through the air, rattled Whalen's bones from behind. He reached for the Glock on his hip. Turned, keeping his back neutral to the bar, seeing the men behind it in his peripheral. Two men approached him from the entrance. One held a bar stool. The other a busted bottle of bourbon, its edges like teeth on a saw blade.

Whalen gritted his teeth, mouthed, "Don't want trouble, just Lang."

One with the barstool said, "Ain't here."

Whalen rolled his eyes, asked, "Where is he?"

One with the stool said, "Some son of a bitch that punched like a mule come in here, cleaned house looking for his sister and a guy we know by Ned. Took Lang. Went to Pete's."

Whalen's arm started to tremble. Motherfuckers, he thought. Spit thickened in the corners of his mouth. He motioned his Glock at the one holding the stool, asked, "You got a name?"

The man said, "Name's Cramp. Why?"

Whalen told him, "Put down the stool. Turn around. You and me's gonna take a ride."

Cramp hesitated, stared at the gun. Dropped the stool. Turned his back to Whalen, who pulled finger cuffs from his belt. Clamped them over Cramp's thumbs. Said, "Gonna show me where this Pete lives. Any one of your buddies gets in my way, I'll finish what that other guy started."

●

Four men holding shotguns stood outside the black-and-gray shack, their dogs chained, waiting for a command. Angus eased one foot on the brake, the other off the gas.

"Think you gonna just drive up this road, these men gonna let you through?" Lang asked from his bubbled lip the shade of eggplant, his hands belted by leather behind him.

Shadows from the trees lining the gravel road spotted Angus's face and the arm that hung out the rolled-down window, and he said, "Pretty much."

"The 'Brook is done started." Burgundy drops fell from Lang's mouth.

Angus told him, "Don't matter."

Lang said, "You fuck with McGill, he'll kill you!"

Angus had been approached years ago, before the accident, to fight in the Donnybrook. Never wanted anything to do with it. The purse was tempting. But too many men he knew who liked to fight, earn extra cash on the side, had disappeared after coming to fight in the Donnybrook. Rumor was if you showed skill, even if you lost, McGill wanted you in his stable to network throughout the counties of backwoods bare-knuckle fighting. Milking your marrow for money regardless of your diminishing abilities, betting for and against his own.

Angus laughed, said, "Maybe he will, maybe he won't."

Lang asked, "You think Ned and this root-headed spinster is worth dying for?"

Angus told Lang, "Done left me for the maggots once. Won't happen twice."

Angus pushed the brake down. Waited. Watched a man walk in front of the Tahoe. Come around to his side, lay a hand next to his arm inside the door. Nod. The other three stared through the passenger's side window. Walkie-talkie static channeled in and out. One of them with teeth the color of piss looked in and chuckled, "The fuck happen to you, Lang?"

Another on Angus's side asked, "You a fighter or onlooker?"

"You tell me," Angus replied, as he grabbed and pulled the guard's wrist, pinning his arm down inside the Tahoe and punching the gas to the floor. "I say I ain't neither one. I's something else entirely."

•

Inside the old barn, Goat and Walkup twisted Liz's arms behind her back while McGill spread her mouth open with metal tongs, glanced inside, and said, "All her teeth is still white. No rot. She can still gag on some cock."

Liz nearly retched at the taste of acidic steel. Pink ran down the corners of her busted mouth.

McGill laid the tongs on the oak table behind him, next to his walkie-talkie, a .38 pistol, a half gallon of Old Grand-dad, and Liz's rucksack of meth and the money she'd made thus far. Screams bounced off the barn from outside. The first fight was coming to an end. McGill said, "Girl, one thing I never get tired of is pussy, regardless of type." He looked over at Walkup, said, "Let Goat hold her. Come around here, see what kind of pussy you'd call her."

Walkup was an ex-carny, had traveled with the county fairs, run the Pick a Ducky, Win a Prize game. Seen and lain with many an unsavory female. He released his grip from Liz's wrist, stepped in front of Liz. Felt one of her hefty mounds. Rubbed his thorny chin, spit brown sludge onto the barn floor. He'd a gray burlap beard and a red bandana over his head. Steel skulls in each earlobe. He turned to McGill, spoke in a slow yodel. "Well, you got your state-fair pussy. They doll up with clown makeup, get out once a year. Thumb a ride from the sticks to the city fair. Get some city dick. Then you got your beat-up pussy. Ones that let they husbands or boyfriends beat on them but still let 'em throw a dick their way. Then you got your trailer-park pussy, which is just an offshoot of white-trash pussy. Some unclean, split-lip bitch whose shit attracts dog-pecker gnats 'fore they even drop they drawers."

Walkup glanced over Liz's shoulder at Goat, who by trade raised goats for milk and meat. He'd cataract eyes, the skin around them hanging like damp shammies. His corn-oil hair was hidden beneath a black trucker's cap with the orange Auto Zone logo faded across the top. Walkup asked, "What kind you thinks she is, Goat?"

Goat spoke with a lisp. "She got them strands running down from her scalp. You know, like that *Clash of the Titans* bitch."

Walkup spit again. Told McGill, "That settles it, boss. She's Medusa pussy."

McGill chuckled. "Then Medusa's gonna get shined up, 'cause she'll be busy on her back trading spread-eagle for a wage the next few nights." McGill winked at Liz. "I take fifty percent off the top. That pays for my time that you wasted, bitch."

The barn door squeaked open. Ned stepped in. Face highlighted by knuckle imprints. A gash about his forehead. Mouth the wrong shade of blue. Tops of both hands open expansions of flesh. McGill laughed. "You win?"

Still heaving, Ned grunted, "Yeah."

McGill said, "Scar tells me this piece of ass travels with you. How the shit you hook up with this feisty broad, Ned?"

Ned grabbed the bottle of bourbon from the table. Turned it up. The walnut-sized knot in his throat ran up and down. He lowered the bottle and said, "Ah, long story short, she and me made a deal at Leavenworth Tavern. Kill her ole man for a sampling of her sours, a cut of the crank she and her ole man cooked."

McGill pointed and said, "Mean that rucksack on the table?"

Ned looked where he had picked up the bourbon. "Yeah, part of that is mine."

McGill smiled and said, "Tell you what, Ned. Win the 'Brook, you can have your half of everything in the ruck. I'll keep the rest for her waylaying my daughter. You lose, I keep it all."

Ned had killed and fucked for what was in that ruck-sack. Damn near got his ass dry-humped by Pete and his gang of retreads. Done paid a thousand bucks to fight in the Donnybrook. Ned was all gums greased the shade of battle, said, "Gonna shit and fall back in it, split-tail son of a bitch!"

McGill's eyes baseballed in size. "You watch your gar-gled tongue, toothless bottom-feeder."

Anger vibrated beneath Ned's feet as, still pumped from the fight, he stepped to McGill, clenched a right uppercut into McGill's gut.

Goat's eyes watered in amazement, and he blurted "Holy fuck!" as he stood paralyzed, in shock.

Walkup backed away from Ned and McGill, wanting no part of either man's menace, and said, "Son of a bitch has got the mad cow in his head."

McGill doubled over. His right hand fumbled for some-thing at his belt. Ned followed up with a left hook into McGill's skull. Dropped him to one knee. McGill pulled a piece of black steel half the size of a road flare from his side. Flung his wrist away from his body and the steel ex-tended into a baton. He swung it into Ned's left shin. Worked it up Ned's thigh. Stood up. Rattled Ned's ribs, jabbed his kidney.

Ned huffed, raised both hands to shield his head. McGill branded Ned's forearms, shoulders, and skull with the metal ASP baton.

Ned screamed, "Motherfucker!" and tried to curl into a protective ball.

McGill panted, stabbed the ASP up and into Ned's stomach, not breaking the skin but taking the rest of Ned's air, and he hissed, "I'd have taken you in long ago. If you wasn't as crooked as me."

Liz's vision kept blurring and clearing. She'd watched the ASP pelt Ned's body like hail on a tin roof. Had felt the tension of Goat's hands loosen. When her vision cleared again, she stomped his feet. Pulled her hands free. Came at McGill from behind. Pushed him into Walkup. Grabbed her rucksack from the table and McGill's .38. Turned around to McGill, who raised the baton with madness in his eyes. He hollered, "Fucking cunt!"

Liz fingered the trigger. Told McGill, "Any man hit a woman deserves double in payback."

Ned's body burned with welts and cherry bruises as he stood up, pushed past Liz, and planted a low right uppercut into McGill's gut. McGill dropped the ASP and hit the barn floor like water breaking from a pregnant woman in contraction.

Walkup and Goat were already on the floor, hands laced over and covering their heads. Then the walkie-talkie on the table buzzed with static, and a man's inflamed voice said, "McGill? McGill? We got a runner dragging ole Cut down the entrance, done busted through the damn gate!"

Liz looked to Ned and asked, "Now what?"

Ned said, "We best get while we still can."

18

Fu sat in the Jeep's passenger seat meditating on needles puncturing skin. Tethered bodies. Inhales and exhales of pleading. Breaking a man's will. Loyalty. He watched Whalen follow yet another piece of greasy bar trash into the house, his pistol pressed into his back.

Cramp asked Whalen, "What's up with you and the fish-eyes in the Jeep, some kind of fetish thing?"

Whalen tapped the pistol against Cramp's skull, reminded him, "Shut the fuck up."

Entering the open door, they found the living room devoid of humans. Gnawed strips of duct tape were scattered across the floor. The interior reeked of soured sweat and sweet honey.

From behind, Whalen felt metal press into his back. A voice followed. "Drop the gun."

Whalen kept his pistol in Cramp's back. "Go 'head, shoot me. I'll separate this old boy's insides."

The voice told Whalen, "Don't make me no difference."

Cramp recognized the voice. Was worried, said, "Come on, Pete. He's looking for Lang and some guy named Angus."

Pete said, "Lang done been here with some man whose face is all uneven. Guess that was Angus."

Whalen questioned, "What about Ned?"

Pete said, "Ned is long gone with some crazy piece of tail. Left us high. Just like Lang and the guy with the uneven face. Now drop the damn gun."

Whalen said, "Fuck you."

Cramp pleaded, "Come on, Pete. He just wants this Angus fella. Where'd they go?"

Pete ignored Cramp, laughed. "Smells like pork tenderloin to me. You a police, ain't you?"

From the hallway a motor hummed. Dodge came rolling down the carpet in his electric wheelchair with Elbow walking behind him holding his privates. Dodge hollered, "The hell is going on in my house?" He held an AR-15 assault rifle across his shot leg, looking like a half-robot killing machine, the blood now dried black down his shin. He lifted the rifle up, said, "Don't wanna answer me?"

Without warning, he opened fire in a sweeping motion across the living room. Elbow squeezed his crotch and screamed, "Fuck you!," pogo-ing deliriously around the room. Whalen ducked, turned his body into Pete. Shouldered him out the open door. Into the yard, onto the ground. Back in the house, Cramp's body opened up with bullets like a pond with rocks breaking its surface. He hit the floor bubbling blood.

In the yard, Whalen and Pete grunted and struggled for each other's weapons. Whalen saw that Pete held a screwdriver, not a gun, and bared his teeth. Bent his wrist against Pete's grip. Forced the Glock's barrel down into

Pete's jaw. Pushed Pete's screwdriver into the other side of his face.

The gunfire ceased. From the house, Dodge cursed. "Son of a bitch jammed up!"

Cramp lay jerking on the living room floor. Looked up at Dodge and gargled, "You shot me, you son of a bitch, you shot me."

Elbow hopped behind Dodge, said, "What you get for bringing strangers to our home."

Outside, Pete lay struggling against Whalen's fifty-year-old strength, his cheek feeling the gun indent it. Spittle webbed like molten taffy when he opened his mouth, saying, "Don't shhh—"

Pete's hands lost their grip when the Glock turned his cheek into a burn, the bullet opening up his skin enough for part of himself to pebble down his jaw. Whalen rolled off Pete. Pete rolled the opposite direction, hands to his face, screaming, "Shit! Shit!"

Whalen got to his knees. Then his feet. His left arm dangled at his side while his right held the Glock up by his ear. His eardrums were shattered from the gunfire.

He watched Pete stagger up and limp toward a sheet-metal garage. Whalen clasped his head three times, trying to get the black-and-white static out of his mind. He lowered the pistol from his ear, aimed it at Pete. Felt something pelt and warm the back of his thigh. His calf. Then his left hand opened up like a firecracker exploding.

Whalen dropped to one knee. Spun in pain to face the open door, where Dodge sat recessed within the house, his mouth agape, brass falling from the AR-15's side chamber.

Whalen raised his Glock. Closed one eye. Split Elbow's kneecap. Lined Dodge in his crosshairs. And returned the same heated jerk.

●

The metal gate V'ed in its center. Busted the Tahoe's headlights and grill. Ramped up over the hood and cab, scratching and scraping metal all the way. Angus kept the gas floored, the engine screaming just like the man whose arm he kept pinned inside the truck.

The man's feet and legs cleaved over the rough curving road, dove up and down with dips and ruts. Angus steered into a curve with his right hand, swerved to within inches of a tree. Released the man's arm. Listened to him grunt and thud into the timber.

Lang, adrenaline-eyed, sat in the passenger's seat and said, "Damn, you might get killed, but you make it worth every second."

The road straightened out into a field of cars. Trucks. Tents. Smoke. People scattered like cockroaches on a crumb pilgrimage. In the distance sat a barn colored black and gray, same as the shack Angus had driven past. Outhouses sat off from everyone, painted identical to the barn and the shack. In the center of the field sat a large square ring lined with barbed wire from top to bottom. A man stood to the side of it on a wooden platform, announcing through a bullhorn the numbers of the next twenty fighters who elbowed and nudged through the waiting others. Onlookers cheered.

Lang said, "They must be starting another round of the 'Brook."

Angus drove around the mass of vehicles that lined the field and asked, "The shit does this Ned drive?"

Lang said, "Beat-to-hell Chevy, last I saw. Orange bed rusted up with a blue-white front end. You best park this beast 'fore they get your ass."

Angus knew that he had a small window of time, that the men at the gate had radioed ahead. They'd be on the lookout for the busted-up Tahoe. He parked it between a Ranger and a Chevette. Left the keys as he clambered out, the sawed-off in his right hand. Jerked Lang from the passenger's side. They walked among rows of cars with men and women lifting bottles and cans, their faces smeared with chicken grease and barbequed venison. Angus noticed men with rifles and walkie-talkies out in the far corners of the field. They were making their way into the crowd of bodies.

Angus wanted vengeance at least as much as the meth. He told Lang, "You see Ned, nod. Mouth his description. All I want is him, my spineless sister, and the dope. You do some dumb shit, I unload both barrels into your skull."

Lang hated Ned as much Angus. Wanted to see him bleed for robbing him and Pete at the bar a few months back. For leaving Pete taped up with them two sadist brothers. But Lang wanted something for all the trouble Angus had brought him, especially for his busted-up bar. He said, "Sure, I'll point him out—for a price. And why don't you unbind this belt from my wrists? Fucking arms is numb."

Angus tapped both barrels down on Lang's neck with one hand. His other hand dug into Lang's arm, and he said, "You're in no spot to barter any deals or get them wrists released. Make toward the ring, distance ourselves from the truck, and I tell you what, I'll let you keep on breathing."

The doors of the black-and-gray barn swung open. Ned limped out holding his shoulder. Liz held a gun in one hand. Rucksack slung up over her shoulder. Lang spotted them. "Look! Up over at the barn! There goes Ned and your mangle-headed sister."

Angus spun Lang to the ground and pushed off through the boozers, joint huffers, bourbon chasers, and crank sniffers. Lang squirmed on the earth, watched Angus disappear as he hollered, "What the shit, man! Unbind my fucking wrists!"

To Angus's right, the man with the bullhorn bayed, "FIGHT!"

In the ring, men slapped fist and knees into one another's bones. Traded gasps of air for knuckles and shins. Skulls cracked. Ribs gave. Skin peeled. Men bled.

Angus cleared the bodies of belligerence and discontent, watched Ned and Liz run through the field toward a line of cedar. He followed with vengeance flowing free as creek water in his bloodstream.

Hauling ass down the entrance road came a roaring, jacked-up red Ford. It slowed, its occupants searching the rows of parked cars for the busted-up Tahoe. Till the driver stopped. Three men from the shack got out. One brought a walkie-talkie to his mouth, the others peered into the Tahoe's windows and anxiously kicked the gravel.

With guns in tow, a pack of McGill's men led leashed hounds through the crowd of onlookers toward the Tahoe. Let the hounds get a scent.

And like the next round of the Donnybrook, the hunt was on.

•

Jarhead's eyes burned from the smoke of onlookers' cigarettes and narcotics. He fanned a hand in front of his face.

Purcell asked, "They ways getting to you?"

"Worst thing about making a living with your hands, you're always surrounded by lives being carved out by abuse. It's how they survive."

Purcell bared five fingers down on Jarhead's shoulder, said, "But not you. You're surviving with your natural-born abilities. Making good out of the decaying class, something your real father never accomplished, though he tried. Thing is, if you win this you still can't save the swarm that is coming for you and your family. But you can find others like yourself and fight for change."

Jarhead asked, "The shit you talking about? How would you know anything about my real father?"

Purcell smiled and said, "I know lots. You'll see."

Somewhere in the distance a truck rumbled. Dogs bawled. In the ring men flattened their knuckles against one another's flesh. Jarhead turned his attention up to the barn. Watched the female with the steady step who'd found the wrong end of the beer bottle, the man who'd won the first round of the 'Brook, and he asked Purcell, "What about them two running from the barn?"

Purcell looked to the barn. Turned back to Jarhead, smiled, and said, "Believe they abilities will soon be omitted."

•

Sweat cropped Whalen's forehead. Blood warmed his lips. Bullet holes bored open his legs. His arms lay motionless at his sides—left hand chopped of several feelers, right hand holding his pistol—with the hard earth cushioning his spine.

The Jeep's door creaked open. Footsteps made their way to Whalen. Fu looked at him through cracked glass. He'd meditated on how he'd make Whalen bleed after they got to the Donnybrook. Found Angus. Liz. Got Mr. Zhong's money. It wouldn't have been with bullets. He glanced back at the Jeep. How would he get to the Donnybrook and collect Mr. Zhong's debt? He'd no idea where he was.

Fu kneeled down, ran his hand over the fingertip-sized bullet holes in Whalen's left shoulder. His body was warm. Chest barely rising.

Behind Fu, Pete stepped from the rusted and warped garage in his boxers and work boots, sticky with dirt, insects circling his frame. He'd a nicked crowbar in his right hand. His other pressed a motor-oil-stained rag into his bullet-burnt cheek. He sucked mucus and said, "You that rotten piece of pork's partner?"

Fu turned around, approached Pete, who questioned, "The shit you think you gonna do, gook, whoop my ass?"

Swinging the crowbar toward Fu's ribs, Pete felt fast,

powerful. He was slow. Fu parted the air with his left hand, hooked Pete's right wrist. Cupped and controlled the crowbar away from his body. At the same time, the fingertips of Fu's right hand drove up under Pete's jaw, the palm turned away from Pete. Fu's fingertips pressed into the soft flesh beneath Pete's chin. Hooked the ridged jawbone. Pushed up. Pulled and unhinged Pete's jaw. The crowbar hit the ground. Followed by Pete's knees. His mouth hung agape with shock. Unable to form speech. Only, "Uhh! Uhh!"

Pete's hands tried to touch his jaw, press it back into place. But the pain was too much.

Fu laughed, told Pete, "You must learn respect for others."

Inside the house, Elbow limped from the bedroom where he'd dragged himself to take cover when Whalen returned fire. Separated his cap. Now the house sat silent as he snuck up the hallway and into the living room. Walls were filled with marble-sized holes. Wood paneling was splintered, and drywall chalked everything. Cotton sprouted from his greasy couch. The television sat shattered. Cramp lay silent, without movement, on the floor.

Elbow jack-legged toward his brother Dodge. Dodge's head slumped to his right shoulder. Drool stringing down his bullet-riddled chest. His eyes, like his chest, were unmoving, and Elbow whispered, "No, no, please, no."

His lips jerked, tears smudged down his cheeks, and he reached a hand to Dodge's face. The flesh was rough and warm. The circulation beneath dissipating.

Elbow ran his hand through Dodge's head of fishing-line

hair, glanced down at the assault rifle across Dodge's lap. Elbow thought, Someone is gonna pay. He pulled each of Dodge's fingers from the rifle. Held it in his grip. Ejected the clip. It was empty.

Elbow glanced through the open door out into the yard. Saw the Asian man standing in front of Pete, who was on his knees. Elbow wrinkled his damp face and muttered, "Who the shit?"

Out in the yard, Fu unbuckled his belt. Stepped to Pete, who still searched for speech. Pete struggled to his feet. Tried to run from Fu, who kicked Pete's ankles from beneath him. He fell flat. Fu pressed into Pete's back. Pete's limbs flailed. Fu drove a palm into the rear of Pete's neck, stopped his flailing. Took each of his arms. Bound them behind him. Wrist over wrist. Pulled him to his feet. Spun him around to face him. Listened to him create god-awful tones. Watched the tears streak dirty down Pete's burnt cheek. Fu grasped Pete's unhinged jaw, pressed both thumbs up into his chin. Rehinged the jaw. Pete stomped his feet into the earth. Spit and hollered, "Fucking-fuck-fuck-fucker!"

Fu laughed. "You will get me to the Donnybrook."

With hands bound behind his back, Pete tried to kick at Fu, to fight him off as he yelled, "Son of a bitch, I ain't getting you nowheres except to a body dump."

Annoyed, Fu forked the fingertips of his right hand into Pete's neck, made him gag, then palmed his shoulder and spun him toward the Jeep. He told Pete, "You will take me now."

Pete tensed up. "Who the shit are you?"

Fu told Pete, "That is none of your concern." And led him to the Jeep's open door.

Then Fu heard a whooping battle cry coming from behind. Before he could turn around, two skeleton-pale arms bear-hugged his body and hard bone dug into his neck.

19

Ned and Liz took to the woods. The rucksack slung over Liz's shoulder bounced as she pushed through the limbs of cedar that scratched her face and arms. Behind her, Ned limped with cramped, bruised muscles, calling out, "Mangy bitch, keep where I can see you and that ruck."

Wondering why she had ever hooked up with this Pez-dispensing piece of shit, Liz turned with the .38 raised. Prodded the barrel into Ned's swelled forehead, told him, "Fucking pariah. You's one that got me into this. Could've sold crank somewheres else."

Ned's eyes crossed taking in the barrel. "Yeah, well, don't forget half that crank and money's mine."

The bawl of dogs came faint behind them, and Ned shouted, "Bitch, get that gun outta my face! McGill and his gang of bastards has got out the hounds."

Liz and Ned came out of the cedar thicket and into deformed formations of gray rock, all shapes and sizes, from house-trailer big to Yugo small. They scrambled and climbed through narrow splits of rock till the land leveled out into soil and moss. It was divided by a barbed fence, a footpath running alongside it. Ned warned her, "Don't touch that. It's running juice."

Liz rolled her plum-lidded eyes and said, "No shit."

"Just follow me." And he stepped to his right. Metal to metal clanked. Ned dropped backward on his ass and hollered, "Goddammit!"

Ned reached with both hands and tugged at his leg, the tibia and fibula chinked and spurred. His boot filled with blood. He'd stepped into an old, rusted animal trap.

Liz shadowed over him. Her face resembled smashed prunes as she took in the pulpy moisture that spread through his jeans. His knuckled lips twitched, and he begged, "Don't just stand there gawking, you morbid cunt. Help get my ankle free."

Liz pig-snorted a laugh and said, "Shoulda watched where you was stepping, you broke-tooth fuck."

Then she turned and walked in the other direction.

Ned screamed, "Don't you leave with that ruck of crank, bitch. Get back here!"

Liz ignored Ned's hail of words. Followed the path along the fence line. Stumbled forward. Her palms slammed the hard surface of rock and soil. She lay in a push-up position and cursed, "The hell?" Twisted her neck, glanced back at her legs and saw a line of clear wire across the path, one end attached to a fencepost, the other end attached to a small metal stake driven into the ground. Before she could move, a slither and hiss came from in front of her. She turned her face to the movement. Spineless coils struck at her from three directions, missing her nose and cheeks by centimeters. Liz went concrete still.

The hounds' barking grew louder. Ned grunted and moaned. Liz watched three copperheads, their tongues radaring out for waves of movement to bounce back. Her eyes followed their tails to the clear wire attached to their scaled ends. Like the trip wire, they were tied to metal stakes hammered into the earth. Ned screamed at her, "Get over here! Get these teeth pulled off my ankle!"

The copperheads coiled their movement and waited. Liz slowly pushed herself backward over the dirt, cedar, moss, and chips of rock. When she felt she was out of striking distance, she arched her back, balanced herself onto her knees, brought her hands to her face. Her insides knotted and twitched as she took in a moment of silence. Exhaled for calm. Heard a familiar voice behind her.

"What's a matter, snake charmer? Them's puny compared to the sizes you're used to." Then she felt a hard heel to her back. It knocked her forward right into the snakes. They struck at her head and neck. Over and over and over. While her hands slapped and she screamed.

Liz's screams ceased, her struggle slowed to a shudder. Snake venom steamed her bloodstream. In agony, Ned twisted his body. Lightheaded, he pleaded with the figure that stood over Liz. "Hey, man, I . . . I'll split what that bitch has in her ruck, just get these damn teeth off my ankle."

Angus watched Liz's flesh swell and bubble with venom. Saw the rucksack over her shoulder. He turned to Ned and said, "You fucking worm, whatever's in that ruck belongs to me."

Ned wiped sweat from his face and groaned, "Huh?"

Angus stepped toward him and said, "I'm the man you

planted a 12-gauge slug into." Angus pointed to his bandaged shoulder stained burgundy. "Left me for possum fodder."

Ned stared at Angus in a sideways glance and said, "Bitch said—"

Angus could hold his temper no more, came down on Ned from behind. Pushed his knee into Ned's back. Placed the sawed-off under Ned's chin, pulled it across his throat. Choked him and gritted, "Wanna hear you gag, you piece of regurgitated meat. Gag! Gag!"

Ned's puffed cheeks shaded fire-engine red. He couldn't breathe, let alone gag. He was dry as a rotted tire lying in a junkyard of heated clay.

Angus quit choking Ned. Stood up. Turned. Grabbed Liz's leg with his free hand. Ignored the pain in his shoulder and dragged her body up next to Ned. Pointed to the rucksack. And said, "That my crank, you spineless bastard?"

Ned rubbed his neck and coughed for air as his eyes watered. He glanced at Liz's frame, now a bloated boil of flesh, told Angus, "Crazy bitch cut me a deal: take you out for a cut of some fresh-cooked crank, a sample of her sours. Shit, I didn't know you. I didn't even know her. Seemed like the deal of a lifetime."

Angus thought about the bark and bite that had opened him up that night, left him inches from death, and his anger wedged even deeper through his veins. He wanted this Ned to bleed and suffer. To wish he was dead.

Squatting down, Angus shoveled the double barrel into Ned's ribs, knocked Ned to his side. Ned's leg tugged within the trap and he coughed and screamed. Raised a hand. Angus threatened, "Ain't leaving you like you left me. I'll make sure every time your chest expands your bladder leaks."

Angus dropped a knee to the earth, kept Ned's body twisted, took clumps of Ned's hair in his free hand, pulled his head back, pushed the sawed-off into his mouth. Ned gagged on the taste of gunmetal. Angus pushed the gun down as far as he could. Smiled and watched mucus run from Ned's bruised and bloody nostrils, Ned's eyes watering as his throat contracted and he tried to retch. Angus wanted to mind-fuck this Ned. He thumbed the triggers of both barrels and said, "Hope that cunt was worth dying for."

Ned vibrated a gargled "NO!" from his throat.

Clicks, and then red dots lit up Angus's body. The growl of hounds seeded the anger that rang in his ears as a voice hollered, "Stop!"

Angus twisted his neck, saw he was surrounded by men bearing high-powered rifles with laser scopes. Cur hounds sat in panted growls. McGill said, "Chainsaw Angus. Son of a bitch!"

Angus said, "This don't concern you."

McGill chuckled. "Don't concern me? That son of a bitch and his whore done caused me enough dilemma. Add that to you dragging one of my men through the fucking entrance, tearing the shit out of my gate. That man's not even good for the hogs to slop on now. You're on my property. Put the goddamn gun down."

Angus jerked the sawed-off from Ned's mouth. Pointed it at McGill. "How about I spread your ass across this acreage with both barrels?"

•

Elbow bit into Fu's neck and squeezed his frame from be-hind. Pushed him forward, sandwiching him into Pete's back. Pete hollered, "You fish-eyed faggot! Quit pressing your prick into my ass."

Elbow ripped at the flesh of Fu's neck. Fu ignored the pain. Dropped his left hand down. Reached behind him. Squeezed Elbow's balls. Elbow spit flesh, hollered, "Yeah! Get you a handful, goggle-eyes!" And started to dry-hump Fu's hand.

Fu twisted his grip. Elbow yelled, "Head-bang this Made-in-China motherfucker, Pete!"

Pete rocked his neck backward, reopened Fu's nose. Blood jetted out of the already swollen lump.

Elbow let go of Fu. Pete turned. Faced Fu. Fu stepped back and drove a quick fist into his throat. Pete's windpipe jammed. His face went pale. Fu stepped forward, crossed his forearms into an X across Pete's throat. Raked his finger-tips down Pete's body like cat claws ripping and burning his skin.

From behind, Elbow kicked the Jeep's door. Bull-whipped the back of Fu's legs. Pete couldn't breathe. Tucked his chin. Raised it. Twisted his head from side to side, try-ing to clear his blocked windpipe. Elbow grabbed Fu's hair with both hands from behind. Jerked him away from the Jeep. Let go when Fu's back hit the ground. Fu went with the momentum. Rolled into a backward somersault. Planted both of his hands on the ground, kept his legs side by side. Planted both feet into Elbow's chest. Dropped him to the ground. Elbow hollered, "Son of a bitch!" Scooted across the ground.

Fu lay in a push-up position, inhaling and exhaling to get his bearings. Pete wormed his hands from the belt that bound them behind him, brought them to his neck. Pinched at his throat till his windpipe popped back into place. He charged Fu, punted his face like a football. Fu's vision fogged, his glasses knocked from his face. His hands went wild, patting the ground for where they lay. Pete stomped down on Fu's hands. Fu caught and cupped Pete's ankle. Pulled him to the ground. Clutched at his body. Rolled him facedown. Pete kicked. Tried to squirm away. Fu's hands dug into the back of Pete's boxers. Tugged on them, baring Pete's pale ass.

Elbow grabbed the crowbar from the ground, stood up and brought the crowbar up over his head. An explosion opened the air. Elbow's chest parted around a hole. Then another explosion and another hole in his chest, a series of unconnected dots. The crowbar hit the earth. Elbow followed.

Behind him, Whalen stood on his knees, bloody. The ache from the knife wound in his thigh was nothing compared to the bullets that had raked his torso. He held his smoking Glock. Finally, he lowered it.

Fu straddled Pete's squirming back. Fu laughed and said, "Assume the slug posture."

He felt for Pete's left arm, cupped his left hand around the forearm, twisted and raised it up, pressed his right hand on the elbow so it wouldn't bend. Then all at once, Fu pushed Pete's arm into his shoulder, dislocated it. He let it flop to the ground beside Pete, who screamed in agony.

Fu did the same to Pete's right arm. Then patted the ground until he found his glasses.

Whalen pushed himself to his feet, felt his body wavering into a numbing shock, dropped the Glock onto the ground. His head was spinning and he fell forward. Fu spun around, caught him. Walked him to the Jeep. Placed him into the passenger's seat. Whalen mumbled, "Donnybrook . . . got to get to the Donnybrook."

The man was in no shape to get anywhere. Fu told him, "I will get us there." He turned and slammed the Jeep's door.

Standing over Pete, Fu watched him grunt and kick his legs, trying to roll over like a fish out of water. Fu kneeled down beside him, said, "I've taken your balance. You cannot go anywhere."

Fu dug his hands into Pete's hair, pulled him to his feet, guided him toward the Jeep.

"Now, you will tell me how to get to the Donnybrook," he told him.

Blister-faced, Pete coughed and spit out, "I ain't telling you shit. Sons of bitches killed Elbow."

Fu palmed Pete's right shoulder from behind, spun him. Pete hollered, "Mother—" Fu's right hand separated the air, gripped Pete's throat. Looking at Pete through busted glasses, Fu said, "You will wish you had not pushed me to this extreme." Fu squeezed till Pete lost consciousness.

•

Pete's vision was a spongy blur. All he could make out were the movements of a dark shape and the scents of motor oil and gas.

188

Pete said, "The fuck?" Wobbled his upper body forward. The separation of his right and left arms from his shoulders brought on a migraine of pain. He tried to move his feet but his shins were bound with fence wire against the legs of the wooden chair in which he'd been restrained.

Pete sat in his boxer shorts, barefoot and defenseless. His vision focused from blurs to the clarity of Fu's outline and he sobbed, "You pet-eating son-of-a-bitch, your buddy killed Elbow."

Fu stood with his back to Pete, tasting the blood that rivered down from his nose to the broken shards of his mouth. He swallowed and said, "We have established this already. Let us talk about what I have found in this rectangular case, what you Americans call a tackle box. Only there is no tackle in it. No fake worms or sinkers or line. Just these curves of wire, hooks."

Fu fingered the jagged pieces of metal from the box. Some long, some short, but all skin-parting sharp. He didn't have his needles. But these would work. He slid several of them into his shirt pocket, then turned to Pete with a long black extension cord in his hand. The cord had been divided into three wires and each was attached to a razor-pointed turtle hook. Pointed the homemade tool at Pete and said, "I will give you one more chance to tell me how to get to the Donnybrook."

Pete sucked mucus and said, "Up yours, slit-eye. Ain't telling you shit!"

Fu closed his eyes. Found that silent state within that wanted to use hurt and create discipline. Opened his eyes, and told Pete, "You will tell me after I've taught you the language of respect."

Pete tried to twist his upper body but it was no use as he slobbered and screamed, "I get loose, gonna get me some Crisco and a Fry Daddy, make your Fu Manchu ass talk ten kinds of fried tongue."

Fu turned, laid the extension cord back on the counter, reached into his shirt pocket for a fish hook, kneeled down in front of Pete, laughed, and grabbed Pete's right foot with his left hand. He thought about forcing Pete's toes back toward his shin, listen to them pop, see how much he could take, but this wasn't about pain, the hooks would suffice, he just needed information. Wanted Pete to talk. He curved the first turtle hook down into the gritty flesh of Pete's heel with his right hand. Fu listened to the callused skin give, watched a drop of blood drip and dot from the heel to the floor, and stared silently as Pete's bladder gave and he screamed, "What the shit you doin' to me?"

Fu asked once more, "How do I get to the Donnybrook?"

•

The butt of the rifle whiplashed Angus's head. His sawed-off hit the ground. McGill's men swarmed him. Held him down. Tied his wrists. Freed Ned's leg. Two men hefted Liz's body from the ground and McGill told them, "Plant a bullet in her brain, we'll take her back and feed her to the hogs, she's beyond repair."

Now Angus and Ned sat side by side in McGill's barn with their hands bound behind them. Liz lay in a feed trough out back, a tiny hole bored into her brain by one of McGill's men.

Outside, nightfall swallowed the countryside. Onlookers sat around fires with the beaten, who held cubes of ice against their abrasions, slugging down bottles of booze to ease their hurt. Minus Ned, all the winners celebrated up at the stables with their trainers, most of them with the same ritual of ice and liquor. They all waited for sunrise, when the next four bouts of the Donnybrook could begin.

McGill held the rucksack open in front of Angus, pulled a baggie of meth from it, and said, "What you're telling me is Ned and your sister left you for dead. Took your dope. You hunted them down to here. Could've been a wasted effort had you pulled that trigger up on the hill and ceased my existence, 'cause my men woulda filled you full of shell shot."

Angus parted his devil's smirk and said, "What's in that ruck belongs to me. No one else. I cooked it. I earned it. It's mine."

McGill closed the rucksack. Laid it on the wooden table next to the whiskey.

Two of McGill's men sat upturning cans of Old Milwaukee with Lang. Passed a pint bottle of whiskey back and forth. Gritty moisture irritated their bodies. Blister-eyed, Lang said, "You sure started some shit, Angus, but it was fun watching you in action."

The barn door creaked open. Two armed men and a girl with a busted nose and Angus's .45 tucked down her waistband entered carrying canvas sacks, drawstrings tied tight around the tops. They closed the door behind them. McGill winked at the girl and asked, "That all of it?"

The girl replied, "All of today's and tonight's betting. Be wheelbarrows more come tomorrow."

McGill told her, "Take it to the back with the rest. Start counting."

The girl nodded. Walked herself and the other two to the rear of the barn. Unlocked a door. In his peripheral vision Angus watched them disappear into the back room. Heard the door bolt from the opposite side.

McGill palmed Angus's face. Smiled. "Don't worry about my money. Worry about what's in that ruck. How bad you want it. 'Cause you owe me a life for the one you dragged through the gate."

Lang said, "Told you not to cross McGill."

Angus jerked his face from McGill's grip and spat, "I owe you shit."

McGill fingered some meth from the baggie, pushed it beneath Ned's nose, and said, "Inhale, Ned. Gotta keep your heart beating till tomorrow." To Angus he said, "Always wondered what became of you after the accident. Sorry about your sister. Sounds like bad skin to be rubbing with anyways. We did you a solid."

Angus was surprised. "You didn't fuck her?"

McGill said, "I don't lay with filth."

Angus said, "Everyone else has."

Ned inhaled the crank into both nostrils and laughed. "Her sours has become spoils."

McGill fingered more meth from the baggie for Ned, looked at Angus, and said, "Here's how it's gonna go. You want your revenge and ruck of crank, you gonna fight for me."

Angus turned his head, tilted it sideways up to McGill, said, "Ain't no doing. I cooked that dope you keep wasting on this lazy swimmer."

Ned snorted hard and started bucking his chair, his leg a bleeding sore wrapped in rags. With razor-thin eyes patted purple, he looked over at Angus and said, "Let my hands loose, I beat you into a plate of mashed taters."

McGill told Angus, "I ain't asking, I'm telling. Come tomorrow, when the sun meets its peak, you and Ned fight in a Hound Round. Whoever is standing when all the blood is fertilizing crushed stone gets to live and keep the ruck."

Angus asked McGill, "The shit's a Hound Round?"

Wired, Ned started to stutter and jerk. His eyelids breached wide, revealed large orbs of busted blood vessels. His gums bled crimson as McGill pressed a palm over his broken lips, told Angus, "Let's just say, even if you refuse to fight, it'll get messy after three minutes."

•

Pete's lips pressed uneven beneath five single bulbs that hung, spread out, from high rafters. His teeth bit down, lockjawed. His arms hung flaccid at his sides. The muscles of his abs and legs rang tight with hurt from the fear of what Fu was doing with the hooks. Only there was little if any pain. Only a prick, then he'd lose feeling somewhere in his body.

Beyond the open door, fireflies lit up the dead shades of night. Dogs barked from far off and crickets violined with Pete's redneck chorus of racial slurs from inside the garage.

One hook started at the ball of Pete's foot, below the middle toe, another curved into the arch, and the third into the heel. The red from Pete's foot started to dot onto the garage's cracked floor, then subsided. The last hook had caused a clear liquid to run from the corners of his sol-dered eyes and mouth, down his chest and abdomen. He'd no control over it.

Fu exhaled with irritation and asked Pete again, "How do I get to the Donnybrook?"

Pete sucked knurled jelly strands back into his nose, unable to comprehend what the Chinaman was doing to him, how these hooks could maybe sting but not really hurt and he tried to spit but coughed, and said, "Daddy always told of them gooks he killed in 'Nam. Said they'd take damn near an entire clip to quit moving. He made me just as tough, you squid-eyed piece of shit!"

Fu smiled, fanned his index finger back and forth, and said, "I find that most amusing, seeing as I'm Chinese, not Vietnamese. Regardless of your ignorance, we will see." He fingered another gold-colored hook from his pocket, lifted Pete's left hand that was weighted from being immobile. Pressing the sharp point into the turnaround between the man's thumb and index finger, Fu bull's-eyed a meridian that caused Pete's left eye to droop, his mouth to sag, and his jaw to drop. He appeared as though his left side was melting.

Pete mumbled, "Fupp you doob too . . . meee?"

"The Donnybrook. You nod, I take out the hook, return your face and speech to normal, you tell me how to get there."

Pete tried to spit on Fu, but could not form, let alone use, the muscles that it took and only drooled even more down his peach-pit chin and fumbled curses that made him sound like a child struggling with his learning curve for speech's consonants and vowels.

Fu was running out of time, had wasted too much on this backwoods miscreant. But in many ways he was impressed by the roughneck's fortitude to take what Fu had given and not be broken.

From behind came the lag of boots stumbling. Turning around, Fu eyed Whalen in the doorway. "Hell you doin' with this pasty fuck?"

Fu positioned himself, lined his torso to go straight into Whalen, to blind the eyes, take the throat. Looked as if he'd tried to sneak up on him. "Trying to break him, get directions to the Donnybrook."

Whalen was beaten and worn, Fu knew this, but somehow the man had dragged himself from the truck, made it to the garage. He watched Whalen use the makeshift counter to balance himself upright, pick up a bright-blue plastic handle that looked like an oversized Maglite with a three-foot white rod connected to it, two rounded pieces of copper at its tip. He stared at Fu, who made a fist with his left, his right loosened, his fingers would segregate the man's center, take away his air. Whalen glanced at Pete, took in the hooks embedded within him, plugged in the device, thumbed a button on the plastic handle. Electricity arced between the copper tips. Fu was ready to kill when Whalen said, "Why the shit ain't you usin' this to loosen his tongue?"

Fu relaxed, saw he was not a threat to him, told him, "It is not about torture, it is about direction."

"The fuck it ain't." Whalen stumbled toward Pete. "I'll treat you like an animal not wanting to follow its herd."

Pete tried to twist his head from side to side but had no control of his body.

Fu gripped Whalen's shoulder. Whalen said, "Let's try it my way." He prodded Pete with the penny-colored tip. Making him dart. Splotched his flesh with a nickel-sized pinch of rubber-tire burn-out. Pete flexed stiff and tried to pull himself from the chair as he tried to scream, but it came out mumbled: "Summ . . . muvvv . . . uhhh . . . bbshhhh!"

Fu removed the fish hook from Pete's hand and Pete's speech returned. His crooked lips parted and he gasped and whimpered. "You go out the way you come . . . hang a right out the end of the drive. Follow Old Engine Road for five miles back . . ."

After Pete told Fu and Whalen how to get to the Donnybrook, he pleaded, "You . . . gonna let me . . . g-g-go now, right?"

Whalen shook his head, turned around, laid the juice zapper back on the workbench, nearly fainted. Fu caught him, propped him in the doorway. Turned back to Pete and began removing the hooks from his body. Returning his feeling with each pull, except for his dislocated arms.

Standing over him, Fu took in the moist lines of Pete's hair that veined across his forehead. The smell of burnt self all around him.

Pete tried to inhale. Got choked. The corners of his mouth appeared greased. From behind, Whalen slurred, "Hell you doin', Chinaman?"

"Thinking how this man who proclaims himself as Pete, how he is either stubborn or disciplined."

Pete puckered his lips. Lined his head to Fu's shape. In his mind he argued with himself. This shouldn't have happened. How did he let it? It couldn't end this way. Bound and beat by two men just as crazed and misanthropic as himself. *No!*

Pete wondered what this slant-eyed man was getting at, whether he'd release him or not. Feeling wrung out, he formed what saliva he could and spit at Fu.

Specks of slobber dotted Fu's face. He forearmed the wet from his complexion. Held an idea in his mind, looked up into the garage rafters. Noticed a steel wire with a clamp-hook hanging above him. It was attached to a come-along that was bolted to a four-by-four stud that ran along the wall. Fu turned away from Pete and started searching about the garage. Found a large military green canvas bag. He opened it. Emptied its contents: soiled and moldy desert-patterned fatigues, combat boots, canteen, and MREs. He grabbed a pair of tin snips from the garage's work-counter. Cut the wire from Pete's shins and chest. Watched Pete pummel to the concrete floor, inhaling his stenched, violet body. Pete's face was creased with tears. He wailed as Fu worked the canvas over his head. Tried to kick and squirm. Fu punched and palmed him, knowing Pete had little left in him, as he worked the bag down over Pete's legs.

Whalen thought Fu was wasting time. "The fuck are you doing?"

Fu bound the top of the canvas bag with more fence wire. Lowered the hook down from the rafter, hooked the fence wire on the bag, and worked the come-along's handle, lifting Pete up from the ground, suspending him into the air as he did all the others. Letting them meditate on all their wrongs, what had brought him to them, a second chance of learning through pain. Conditioning. And he told

Whalen, "I think he will make a good prospect, maybe I'll come for him later."

"Prospect for what?"

"My business."

As Pete hung from the rafter, his words were garble-tongued. Fu stood in the garage's open door, helping Whalen to his feet, led him back to the truck, distanced himself from the pebbles-in-a-blender tone of a possible student.

PART III

PANDE-
MONIUM

20

Saturday of the Donnybrook brought a heat wave of swollen hands, black eyes, and hulled lips. The fourth free-for-all of fresh bodies had entered the ring. Beat on one another till only one remained standing in frayed cutoffs and slick-bottomed boots. Flecks of blood and bone shadowed the spiderweb tattoos that coiled up each of his ball-bat forearms, twisted and tied into the railroad spikes that nailed into his right and left shoulders. They had been inked by a tattoo-artist friend wanting the same thing he wanted, getting out of the Kentucky hills. It was Jarhead Johnny Earl.

Goat and Walkup stood with Angus while Ned sat tied in the barn, getting fingernails of meth from Scar. Angus watched McGill pat Jarhead on the back and say, "Got two more free-for-alls, then get to see you fight for a lot of crumpled green, boy."

Jarhead hadn't come all this way robbing, smuggling, and listening to the prophecies of a backwoods soothsayer only to be treated like a child. He told McGill, "Ain't your boy."

McGill squeezed Jarhead's trap and said, "Johnny Earl,

you win Sunday, you'll be whatever I say you are. Make more money than your blue-blooded ass can count."

Angus laughed. "Win it all, Johnny Earl. Let McGill draw you like a turnip, leave you to bask in the heat."

Purcell had already figured out who Angus was from his visions. Jarhead sized him up like he did every man he saw. Long hair pulled tight over a shattered-glass complexion. His arms were bound behind his back, forcing his shoulders and pecs to flex. For a man who had to be every bit of forty, his body looked racehorse hard.

McGill introduced them. "Johnny, this here is Chainsaw Angus. Once a bare-knuckle legend. Never beaten. Only man to ever beat—"

"Ali Squires." Jarhead knew the legend, knew all the men Angus had beat. And he'd be happy to have a shot at him. But rumors had said Angus no longer fought. Still, he was glad Purcell wasn't lying, wasn't just a crazy shithouse recluse. McGill smirked. "Good, you know his reputation. Now, go get yourself some food and drink. Relax for tomorrow. Get ready to watch Angus come out of retirement."

Jarhead's swollen eyelids lit up like fluorescents. He said, "Coming out of retirement?"

And sarcastically McGill said, "Yeah, putting wheels back on the buggy. Gonna let him take us for a wild ride."

Jarhead said, "Can't wait to see the legend in action." Winked at Angus, stepped away. Met the graying, long-haired Purcell, who'd a backpack slung over his shoulder.

The old man caught Angus's attention. Shot him a smile, a respectful nod. Then he and Jarhead disappeared into the mass of smacking lips, smells, swells, and slurps.

McGill told Goat, "Get Manny and his Mutts. Bring Ned out. Then get back to Walkup and Scar, keep an eye on the money." He told Angus, "Time for the ring."

Angus kept a granite face. They'd fed him grilled venison, blackened potatoes from foil. Let him wash it down with water, a few beers. He'd slept on the barn floor with Ned on the opposite side. Woken before sunrise with the shakes. He hadn't had a bump in days. Had the itch. He'd told McGill, "I get my shit back, put as much road between us as possible." That was a small lie. He would—just as soon as he figured a way to get from the ring to the barn's back room. Because the way Angus saw it, no man had ever been stupid enough to cross McGill at the 'Brook, knowing if he got caught it'd be his burial.

After all his suffering, cooking and selling meth to the lost lives swimming in narcotic sludge, this was where he'd ended up. Being forced to use his fists in some backwoods cockfight with more lives just as lost as his own. His second chance wasn't the meth, it was McGill's money.

McGill chuckled. "How long has it been? Two, three years? Think you still got it?"

Angus didn't blink, said, "Something you'd never understand is that a real fighter never loses his skill. His instinct. Just pray you don't brush up to me without these rigs around my wrists."

McGill squinted and said, "Is that spite or disrespect? You making a threat?"

Angus told him, "I don't make threats. I offer moments to reconcile one's shitty choices."

•

The wire gate opened. Onlookers cheered, "Blood! Blood! Blood!"

Shirtless, wearing work boots and faded carpenter pants, Angus entered the barbed ring. He stood six feet two inches. His oil-colored locks with hints of ash were raked over his head, woven into his usual braid. His back, shoulders, chest, and abs were lean, striated rib eye over brick, his body graffitied with the names of those he'd beaten outside of taverns and logging camps.

Angus clenched his tattooed fists. Did a few squats to loosen his knees, threw quick jabs, hooks, elbows, and knees at the air. Keeping his muscles warm while burning holes through Ned.

Across the ring, Ned's face was redolent of a bushel of peaches opened up by buckshot and left to decompose in the summer sun. Flies and gnats accompanied him as he limped back and forth, rags wrapped about his wounds and an axe-handle splint on his leg, his hand trailing the gauged fencing for support.

Ned tried to make a fist with his free hand. Squeezed. The movement brought a jagged tremor that traveled down to his balls. Felt as though a hammer had smashed them on a cast-iron anvil. But the meth in his veins ate up the pain.

In each of the four corners of the cage was a three-by-three plywood door that remained closed. Behind each kneeled a man restraining a hound frothing from pink and black gums for the taste of human. Waiting for the fight to begin, the dogs as anxious as the onlookers for the three-minute window to pass and the door to open.

Four men entered the ring carrying lidded ten-gallon buckets. Two walked toward Angus, the other two split off toward Ned. They removed the bucket lids. Dumped the contents on Angus and Ned. Twenty gallons of steaming cow's blood. The dogs, and the onlookers, grew even more agitated.

The Hound Round rules had been laid out for Angus and Ned the night before. Two fighters had three minutes to beat each other till one was without fight. If both men were still standing after three minutes, then a hound was released—turning the fight into man versus man versus hound. If another three minutes passed and both men and hound were still mobile, then another hound was released. The key was beating an opponent before the three-minute mark. The round went on till one fighter, on two legs or four, was standing alone.

The men with buckets walked out of the ring. Angus and Ned stood bloody and greased. The gate was bolted. A man with a bullhorn and black hair cut like Moe from the Three Stooges stood on a podium outside the ring and yelled, "FIGHT!"

•

After sleeping in the Jeep overnight, Fu navigated through Orange County, following the curved and broken roads Pete had described to him. Whalen rode shotgun, shirtless, his pale body bludgeoned by gunfire to the shade of ruby. He dozed in and out.

Inside the rotted house with a tar roof where one man

lay dead on the floor and another sat dead in a wheelchair, each bullet-holed like the house's interior, Fu had searched through hard and crusted towels for something clean. Found some shirts and, in the bathroom, bottles of rubbing alcohol and peroxide. Cleaned his own wounds in the sink.

In the Jeep, Fu ripped Whalen's soiled shirt from his body. His left shoulder had been nicked, the right side of his chest and lower abdomen gashed. Fu knew the wounds were not as severe as they appeared. He tore the shirts from Elbow's house into strips. Dabbed the strips in peroxide, blotted the wounds, watched them fizz into a yellow liquid. Wiped and repeated. Then he poured the alcohol over each wound.

Whalen's eyes blinked open from the burn. He tried to move his right arm, feel for the pistol that wasn't there, but his body was stiff like Heath English toffee. He felt as though he'd crumble. He said "My gun, where's—"

Fu's left hand cupped Whalen's wrist, his right held the alcohol, and he instructed him, "Don't move."

Whalen blinked a few more times. His mind was foggy. Then he recognized Fu as the hitchhiker he'd saved, began to remember what had happened, quipped, "You ain't no fighter like I ever seen."

Fu blotted the alcohol and said, "Have you seen a lot of fights?"

Whalen said, "Had my share of tavern and trailer-trash disputes. Nothing like that *Billy Jack* shit you's doing."

Fu wrinkled his forehead and inquired, "Billy Jack?"

Whalen said, "Never mind," paused, thinking how he'd found Fu bruised and bloody alongside the road. He asked,

"This Donnybrook, I never asked what kind of business you have there."

Fu set the alcohol on the floorboard between Whalen's feet, said, "I never offered." Fu thought how he'd first wanted to test Whalen, see how he carried himself, had thought about how he'd kill him after he'd gotten Mr. Zhong's money. But Whalen had saved him from the man called Elbow. Fu no longer viewed Whalen, the peace-keeper, as a threat. And he didn't know if he had any lessons to teach him. As much as it surprised him to think it, maybe even the opposite. He told Whalen, "I am collecting a debt. When I first found the man who owed us, he told me his sister stole the money, and that she was headed for this Donnybrook."

Whalen's heart raced. He clenched his fist and blurted, "Angus!"

He ignored the ache, tried to lift himself from the seat once more. His spine cracked and popped and Fu's left palm offered a soft touch with an unknown force behind it. Whalen coughed, tried to catch his breath, and Fu said, "You know this man who goes by Angus?"

Whalen sat trying to find the air Fu had knocked from him and he gasped, "Yeah . . . he's a meth cook and . . . a murderer. He's why I's headed to the Donnybrook."

Fu sensed something in Whalen's tone and said, "I would not trust this man. I watched him fight. I thought he was honorable. I made a deal with him that he would lead me to his sister and he would repay the money. He would get to keep his drugs. But he double-crossed me along the way. This Angus, he will double-cross you too."

Whalen closed his eyes, thought about the guilt he'd carried all these years. The confession to Reese. Maybe he should've went about it a different way, but Whalen had grown tired of seeing Reese raise those kids, tired of hearing Reese bitch about how he couldn't sire a child that wasn't unmalignant or slow. When the fact was he'd yet to sire a child at all. Day before Reese went mad, over a few drinks, Whalen had told him, them kids—Tate, Doddy, and Gravel—all of them were his. And he would be taking them, the farm, and Azell from Reese.

Whalen felt weak and useless. Too fucked up to hunt down this Angus and kill him. He opened his eyes, looked at Fu and his beat complexion. Realized his redemption lay in this man who was more than he appeared to be. "Double-cross? He murdered my *son*. My only chance of seeing my lineage seeded."

Fu questioned, "Son?"

Whalen took in a deep breath and said, "Angus and his sister are connected to a double murder. I got a tip Angus was headed to the Donnybrook, but before coming down here to Orange County, I stopped by my family's abandoned farm where my son, Gravel, lived. Found him dead in the farmhouse kitchen. Along with a mess of supplies for cooking meth. Found Angus's wallet in a back bedroom."

Whalen paused, tears flicked down his face, and he said, "The son of a bitch killed my boy and squatted in the farmhouse, cooked his crank. I'd no intentions of arresting Angus, and now I'm in no shape to do what I wanted."

Whalen had grabbed Fu's wrist. Thought of Doddy, his pregnant daughter, knocked up by a neighbor boy, she'd been taken from him that day Reese had found the madness, and with hay fever eyes and gritted teeth, Whalen had said, "I want you to make this killer disappear like he did my legacy."

Now Fu turned down the entrance to the Donnybrook. Whalen lay motionless in the passenger's seat. Three men stepped from the black-and-gray guard shack. Fu slid the Jeep into park, opened the door, and approached the first guard, who was reaching across his body and mouthing, "Hold on there, you split-eyed son of a—"

21

In the center of the square ring, red channeled down Angus's head, chest, and arms like extra arteries. He counted Mississippis in his head, keeping check on the hounds' three-minute window. His hands raised at his temples, elbows tucked in guarding his ribs, his left foot forward, he created an imaginary line that segmented Ned's body into halves.

Animal rot coated Ned's beat frame. Unbalanced, he pillowed his temple with his right hand. Moved forward, pumped a weak left jab at Angus's nose.

Angus read Ned's movement before Ned knew what he was executing. Angus dropped his head down, pressed his chin into his chest. Ned's knuckles mashed into the top of Angus's skull, the sound of walnuts being broken open. Angus raised his head, smiled, pivoted on the ball of his rear foot. Quick as death, he right-hooked Ned's inner right forearm before Ned could pull it back, pressed forward, and turned the right hook upside down. Pumped an uppercut into Ned's solar plexus.

Ned deflated. Dropped to his knees. Heaved cherry red.

Drunken swells of, "Goddamn!" And, "Beat that bastard! Beat that bastard!" erupted from onlookers.

Midday heat weighed down on Angus, and he huffed, "Thought you'd more gas in your tank than that." Angus cupped Ned's moist skull in his left hand, pulled Ned's face into his right knee.

Jarhead watched from outside the ring, leaned to Purcell, and said, "I came to fight, win the money, not watch this Angus walk through some spent meth-head. This ain't no competition. This is just sick."

Purcell slid the backpack off his back. Unzipped it. Rested his grip around the pistol that lay in the bottom of it, and told Jarhead, "It's how McGill works. Man's always thirsty to see others in pain. Brings him pleasure and money."

Angus released Ned's dewy locks, stepped to his right, came down, sliced Ned's right temple with a left elbow. Added another cut to Ned's wilted complexion.

Ned hit the rocky ground. Angus spit on him. Exhaled, "Where's that liquid courage you had that night you blistered me with a slug, pinched my crank?"

Ned chewed on clumps of regurgitated self, swallowed enough juice to refill the corroded tank that the meth had left strung out. He spread his hands across the gritty ground, pushed himself up to his knees, and, scattering pieces of rock, charged at Angus with his head down. Grunting and slobbering, he rammed his right shoulder into Angus's stomach.

Angus took the hit, exhaled, "Uhh!" The momentum doubled Angus over Ned's back. Angus wrapped his arms around Ned's center, hefted him straight up into the air and dropped him straight down. Ned screamed, "Shiiiiiiiit!" as his neck and shoulders crunched and gave.

Onlookers stomped their feet and whooped, "More! More! More!"

Ned lay quivering, and Angus kneeled down, told him, "None of this would've occurred if you'd left well enough be. I ain't gonna kill you. Just make you wish I would end your life." Angus motioned a thumb outside the ring at McGill, who sat in a lawn chair, bug-eyed and salivating, yelling, "Kill that son of a bitch! Stomp his fucking face!"

To Ned, Angus said, "When I'm done with you, gonna do the same to that glutton McGill. Take all his money."

A hopeless, maniacal gleam in his eye, Ned's beat lips spewed, "I hope you try, you ugly cur. McGill, these people, they will cut you up, Chainsaw—" He spluttered into bloody, crazed laughter.

Angus had counted to one hundred and eighty Mississippis in his head. Told Ned, "Save it, your time's up. Hope them hounds like to eat shit." He reached out, pulled Ned's arms with both hands. Dragged him to his feet. Made him stand. Ned gave a pain-filled scream as the plywood door from the corner behind Angus opened up.

Outside the ring, anger and testosterone oxidized Jarhead's insides. He couldn't believe what he was about to see. Lowered his head to Purcell and said, "I do man verses man. Man verses hound, I don't do."

Purcell chuckled, held Jarhead's eye, and said, "Any man wants to fight for McGill has to do whatever he says or end up worser than these two."

Jarhead bounced those words around in his head. Fighting to prove who the better gladiator was, that was one thing. But he wouldn't be the slaughterhouse butcher for a deviant like this.

In the ring, claws tacked across granules of stone. Angus held Ned up, grunted and twisted around, pushed Ned in front of him, used him as a shield.

Coal-colored spots stabbed the hound's gray coat. It came growling, its caramel ears bouncing till its stride ended at Ned. Who tried to raise his salved hands. But his arms held no strength. He was spent. The rabid hound's teeth were equal to straight razors, shadowing Ned's complexion a deeper hue of garnet. Opening wounds trying to scab. Mixing them with new ones.

Not wanting to be next, Angus stepped over the hound's back. Sat on him like a saddled horse. Locked his legs around the beast's gut, squeezed his thighs, crushed the hound's insides. The hound yelped and growled. Angus slid his forearms in front of the hound's throat, hugging and pulling it toward his chest, rested his chin on the hound's head. Leaving no gap between his body and the hound's. Angus felt as one with the hound, its heart pounding with his own, rattling against the bones of his chest. Angus closed his eyes, pushed his hips forward, arched his back. Pulled the hound's head with him. Bones parted from joints, tendons lost their elasticity, and the only beating heart Angus felt was his own.

The men and women screamed, beyond vehement, they were a sunburnt coil of frothing bloodthirst. They started to shake their cans of unopened beer. Popped the tops. Arcs of white foam shot into the fenced ring and onto Angus.

Winded, Angus ran his tongue around his lips, tasted the foam and blood that freckled and smeared his frame, counted two hundred and forty Mississippis in his head, took in the violent crowd still hollering, "More! More! More!" He hadn't felt a rush like this since fighting in the logging camps.

At Angus's feet, Ned lay mauled. The slight rise and fall of his chest contrasted with the hound beside him, still. Behind Angus, the gate unbolted, and McGill stepped into the ring with the rucksack of crank over his shoulder.

Angus turned, approached McGill and the four olive-skinned men that spread out behind him. The dog handlers. They'd long black hair and thick, ungroomed goatees, with blue bandanas wrapped around their heads, the darkest skin in a fifty-mile radius. Their shirtless arms and chests were heavily inked with cracked skulls, the number seven, fighting dogs. Each rested his hand on a pistol with an extended double clip pushed down into the waistband of his chinos. The leader, the one whose tattoos crawled up onto his face, spoke. "This *puta* kill Stone Man."

Angus regretted nothing he had done to Ned. But he did regret the dog. And was curious to see how McGill would handle this.

McGill was all teeth as he spoke over the onlookers, whose excitement had only grown more uncontrolled. "Save it, Manny, you still got three left. This bastard just upped the stakes. Gonna replace Ned in the 'Brook tomorrow. Don't you worry, you'll get paid for your precious dogs.

And then some." He slapped a wad of cash in the gang-banger's hand, and the three of them slunk back, mollified.

McGill pulled the rucksack from his shoulder, offered it to Angus, and said, "Here's your crank. Go get blasted so you can make me a mint on side bets tomorrow, Chainsaw."

Angus stared at the rucksack of crank, thinking of all the savagery it had brought: a dead pharmacist, a dead backwoods man in a dress, a beat gook and beat bartenders, dead Liz, Ned barely audible with a lifeless beast beside him. Angus smiled as he saw his opening. Told McGill, "Time to reconcile your shitty choices."

•

Just as the first guard reached across his body for the holstered .45 H&K pistol, Fu heeled his right foot into the guard's forearm, trapped it across the man's stomach. Fu's left hand flowed like a whip, walloped the guard's right temple. His right palm came like an uppercut beneath the guard's jaw. Rattled and chipped the guard's teeth. Fu doubled-palmed the dazed guard's chest, knocked him backward into the second guard, who'd pulled his pistol. A shot sounded and a bullet ripped a hole in the first guard's lower back. "Fuck!" the man yelled.

Fu dropped to the ground and spun to his left, sweeping the third guard's legs from beneath him. His head of Willie Nelson–style locks slammed onto the rocky earth, sent an echo throughout his frame. He went stiff. Fu stayed low to the ground, hammered the man's nose and mouth. The guard's limbs thrashed and Fu pressed his right forearm into the guard's Adam's apple till his stiffness ceased.

Fu lurched low, his left and right arms spread away from his body like wings. The second guard stepped toward him with his pistol, and Fu sprang up from the ground. His left hand formed a claw, came down on top of the guard's skull, torqued it down into Fu's right hand, which came palm up like an offering, the ridge of his hand knifing the guard's throat.

The guard went red-faced and dropped his pistol. His hands grabbed his throat. Fu spun behind him, offered left-right hammer punches to the guard's kidneys, worked his way up the spine till the guard hit the ground like a suicide jumper to street pavement. Fu stepped back to the Jeep, got in, and shifted into drive.

●

Earthy lines split across McGill's forehead as he questioned, "Kind of shit you spitting?"

Angus moved like the wind, rooted a steel toe into McGill's gut. McGill dropped the rucksack. Doubled over. Angus slapped the back of McGill's head down into his left knee. Drove him backward into the quartet of gangsters. Gave Manny a straight right to his jaw. Pulled Manny's pistol from his waist with his left. Pushed it into his fat mass of a nose and pulled the trigger. Eyes, lips, and cheek diced across McGill and the *cholos*.

The onlookers chewed on crazy and hollered, "Mother-fucker shot Manuel!"

From the far corners of the surrounding field, the dozen men who guarded for McGill came running toward the ring. The other ten men who watched the fights and took wagers from the onlookers started to push through the crowd.

The Mutts reached for their pistols. Angus reached down for McGill's head of hair. Pulled McGill up into a headlock with his right arm. Flexed his biceps. Pinched and pulled McGill's larynx in the bend of his elbow. McGill was ripe-faced and gagging, a pistol jammed into his ear. His eyes doubled in size as he looked at the bangers pointing their guns at him and Angus, and he rasped, "Don't fucking shoot . . . you . . . ignorant wetbacks!"

Purcell removed his hand from the backpack, bringing with it a shiny piece of steel. He slung the pack back over his shoulder, nudged Jarhead, and said, "You starting to see you didn't just come here to fight?"

Jarhead muttered, "I seen enough."

Purcell said, "Like it or not, we gotta help Chainsaw Angus." And he propelled Jarhead through the crowd, into the ring.

McGill turned his neck left to right, loosened Angus's clench, and spat out, "Release those fucking hounds!"

McGill's men fought through the crowd, who started tossing full bottles and cans of booze at the ring, along with chunks of grilled chicken, goat, and venison. Their screams crescendoed. "Fight! Fight! Fight!"

From behind Angus, the plywood doors at the other corners of the ring opened. Angus retightened his hold around McGill's neck and growled, "You rotten bastard."

Three oversized hounds came at Angus. Two stood their ground, watched the third drill into the muscle of Angus's right calf. Break his skin. Savor the cow's blood that coated his body. Angus tried to kick the dog from his calf, but the dog jerked his leg like a rag from side to side. Tested his balance.

One of Manny's bangers accidently fired a round at Angus. Missed and grazed McGill's chest. McGill hollered, "You stupid son of a bitch!"

Angry onlookers screamed, "They shot McGill!" Everyone started elbowing, pushing, and punching, creating a drunken and doped mosh pit that stomped anyone who hit the ground into a fevered mucilage. And McGill's men were right in the middle.

Before another cartridge could be spent, Jarhead came into the ring, leveled one of the bangers with a punch to the kidneys from behind. Reached over the next gangster's shoulders with a palm to the throat. Purcell cleaned up behind him, kneeled down, hammered the first fallen in the face with the butt of his gun and took his pistol. The third met Jarhead's hooking fist at his temple and hit the ground.

Purcell and Jarhead watched Angus release McGill to the fizzing hound that lockjawed his leg. Angus punched the pistol into the top of its skull, pulled the trigger. Bark and bite sundered into chunks. The other two hounds growled and waited for Angus to approach.

Jarhead hollered, "Look out!" But it was too late.

Angus turned right into McGill, who buried a thumb into Angus's unbandaged wound. Angus pounded the butt of the pistol into McGill's wrist. Then brought it across McGill's face.

McGill shook his head. Licked the ooze from his lips. Raised his fists to Angus.

Angus ignored his pain, laughed, pushed the pistol into his waistband. He wanted to punish McGill. He jabbed McGill's chest wound, calling up fresh waves of blood. McGill dropped his hands to his chest. Angus balled his fists into McGill's shirt. Pivoted his right foot, leaned, and swung McGill into the lunging hounds behind him.

McGill stumbled to the ground with, "I'll feed you your fucking—"

And then the hounds spread his threats over the rocky ring like oil staining pavement.

Angus pulled Manny's pistol from his waist. His left shoulder oozed and mixed with the cow's blood and animal fat that dressed his body. He looked down at the gangsters scattered on the ground in front of him like dumped-out cans of Ol' Roy Dog Food. Knelt down, felt the ache of his right calf that was chewed gum. He pulled a pistol from one of the convulsing wounded, stood, pushed it into his waistband. Faced Purcell and Jarhead. Each was untrusting, burning stares through the others.

Outside the ring, McGill's men were limp slabs of muck beneath the crowd's footing as the onlookers bloodied one another with bottles and fists. Purcell parted his lips, this time with a question. "Now what?"

Angus smirked, he was confused by the old man, and Jarhead, a fighter who'd threatened to beat his face in but now wanted to help him. Angus turned to Purcell and said, "My experience with strangers helping strangers is, they always have a personal motivation."

Purcell replied, "Ain't got time for your past philosophies of how one man wrongs another. Some dicks is crooked, others is straight, but they can all be used for fucking."

Three onlookers stumbled through the open gate and into the ring. One hollered, "Fuckers is gonna pay for what you done to McGill!"

Angus raised his pistol, germinated the air with each man's complexion while telling himself he wasn't leaving without getting to the barn, taking McGill's money. He sized up his options. The odds of three men fighting their way to the barn were better than the odds of one. He needed the other two for that, but nothing else. He swatted at the flies buzzing around his head and said, "McGill's take from the 'Brook is in the barn." He paused, assaulted Jarhead with his eyes, and said, "Know you didn't come here to fight, leave empty-handed. You won't if we make it to the barn."

Jarhead didn't trust Angus, could read his manner. He looked to Purcell, who held a pistol in each hand. Then nodded to Angus and said, "Lead the way."

•

Fu sat watching the chaos unfold. Nudged Whalen and said, "You stay in Jeep. I will find Angus. Fulfill our agreement." He stepped from the Jeep. Made his way into the chaos of men and women blistering one another with fists, bottles, and sticks. Fu punched, palmed, and snapped his way toward the ring. In the furious swirl no one seemed to take special notice of him, but Angus, fighting to get out of the ring, caught his eye from a distance and he came up short. Fu felt hands reaching for his shoulders. In one motion, he spun around with his left arm circling over the top of the man's forearms, coming up beneath the arms, pulling them tight to the left side of his rib cage as if flexing his biceps. Fu spread his legs shoulder-width apart and dropped below the man's center of gravity while his left forearm applied upward pressure, arm-barred the man's elbows. The arms gave and the onlooker screamed.

Fu released him. Felt a bottle shatter over the rear of his skull, then a punch to the ear, a kick to his right leg, then to his left, then another punch and another kick and another bottle and he dropped to the earth.

•

Angus started out into the pandemonium. Men and women screamed, "He's the one that fed McGill to the hounds. Beat his ass!"

Angus tried to save his ammunition in case McGill's men were guarding the money in the barn, used his fists as much as possible while dodging the drunken with their broken bottles and makeshift clubs. Jarhead and Purcell battled behind him, punching and elbowing the sotted and stumbling. Taking a punch or a knee from out of nowhere every few steps.

A broken bottle swept Purcell's ribs, cut through his shirt. He turned and palmed the fresh wound. Jarhead fisted the snaggletoothed bottle wielder in the gut.

A piece of wood hit Angus's right arm. He shouted, "Inbred bastard!" And dug the fingers of his right hand into the onlooker's eyes. Kicked him into the other onlookers and kept fighting.

Making it to the barn, Angus shouldered open the door. Jarhead was one step behind him. Purcell was last, keeping pressure on his wounded rib cage. He slammed and bolted the door, turned to Angus, and asked, "Where's it at?"

Angus pointed to the rear of the barn, where aged two-by-sixes made up a closed door to another room. Light bounced beneath it. A female voice shushed other voices with a loud, "Quiet!" Shadows creaked the planked flooring on the other side of the door. The female voice called out, "Daddy McGill, that you? The hell's going on out there?"

Angus pointed the handgun he'd pulled from Manny and splintered the gray wood with each pull of the trigger, the sound of the gunshots rattling Purcell and Jarhead. When the screams echoing from the room ended with the thud of bodies hitting the floor, Angus quit shooting.

Dried blood flaked from Angus's sweaty forehead, and he acted fast, kick-stomping the door open. In the back room, he stood with his pistol smoking and smiled at the slabs of chip board overtop sawhorses, five-gallon buckets pushed beneath for chairs. Crumpled sacks lay on the floor. Fluorescent lighting overhead outlined the stacks of crumpled bills banded together on top of the makeshift table. It was McGill's take from the 'Brook.

To the side, next to a rusted cast-iron wood stove, three men and a woman lay painting the slatted floor with themselves. The men were still alive. Goat had been shot in his right thigh. Walkup, in the ear. Lang in the gut. Scar lay motionless. Ragged blond hair clung to her face like strips of raw bacon, mascara in Alice Cooper–style circles around her eyes. Her chest lumped out a bloody Drive-By Truckers

T-shirt with a cartoon picture of an old-timer carrying a pick.

Angus stepped toward the three bleeding men. One looked up at him and pleaded, "Please don't shoot me no more. Take what you want. McGill's Bronco is out that back door, keys is in it. Just don't—"

Angus smiled and shot them without contrition.

Behind him, Jarhead's and Purcell's ears rang as they inhaled the fresh gunpowder and smoke that hovered in the air. Jarhead burst out with, "Didn't have to shoot them. Already said to take what you want. Even told you McGill's Bronco is out back."

The barn walls shook under the crowd's fists.

Angus looked at the three pulpy-faced men who lay limp on the floor, sizing up his options again, knowing he'd a way out. He said, "No, I didn't need to, just like I don't need to split McGill's money with either of you."

Angus spun around to Jarhead, his gun pointed at the lone figure.

But Jarhead's fists were already coming at Angus tight as sledgehammers, ready to shatter the leathered barbarian's skull. He planted a left hook into Angus's right hand, knocked the gun from his grip. Threw a blinding right cross that caught Angus on the chin, knocked him back across the makeshift table of money that scattered across the floor like birdshot.

Angus blinked his eyes wide, saliva the shade of rosewood dribbling down his chin, and got out, "You punch like a mule. Let's see if you take one like a man or a bitch." And sprung forward with a right-shoulder feint.

Jarhead's left hand pawed against his temple, anticipating the attack. He bobbed his head to the right, believing the feint was a punch to his left. Angus cut the air at ten o'clock, swung the bottom of his left fist down. A hammer fist depressed the cartilage of Jarhead's nose, then a right vertical punch parted Jarhead's left eyelid like hot asphalt.

Jarhead blinked red, tried to step back. Angus came with a low right roundhouse kick, frogged the muscle of Jarhead's left thigh. For a split second, Jarhead's leg turned to a bed of eight-penny nails. He shifted his balance to his right leg, slapped the air with his right hand, delivered a side-palm to Angus's left temple, planted his left foot, and cut up the center of Angus's body with a left uppercut to the throat. Angus stutter-stepped backward. Coughing and tearing up, he quipped, "Sneaky motherfucker."

Jarhead's left hand guarded his chin. His right hung loose in front of him. His sight was damped by moisture and blood. His lungs heaved. The air he pulled in felt like frosted straight razors etching new expressions of hurt beneath his rib cage. Angus was a black blur, his left and right arms spread like he was hugging a redwood. He slammed his palms against Jarhead's ears and popped his eardrums.

Sound was the needles pricking Jarhead's mind as he felt for Angus's wrists. Angus gripped each of Jarhead's ears, sledged his cranium down onto Jarhead's. The echo of blackness waved to the back of Jarhead's skull, sent all those needles clacking down his spine. His knees buckled, his eyes did an undertow, and he swam into unconsciousness.

Purcell stepped to Angus with his pistol leveled, pulled the trigger, click-click-click. "Son of a bitch!"

Angus slapped the pistol from Purcell's grip, knuckled his eye, knocked Purcell to the floor. He said, "Mother-fucker, try to shoot me? You sit tight, old-timer. I'll get to you after I bloody your boy a bit more."

Angus straddled Jarhead's limp form, laughed as he drove one fist after the next into Jarhead's face.

The back barn door creaked opened.

Angus turned to the beat, cut, and pulpy outline. "How the shit—?"

Fu stepped into the barn, bent, and rolled sideways. His legs cartwheeled up into the air coming forward. Fu's left foot came down on the barn floor, the shin of his right leg came down across the back of Angus's neck. Knocked him facedown on top of Jarhead.

Purcell sat in awe, saying, "The hell, never had no reckoning of you."

Angus tried to shake the cobwebs from his head, push himself up off of Jarhead.

Fu stepped on top of both men, pressed into Angus's back, and twined his left arm over and under Angus's left arm while his right arm came around Angus's throat, cut off his air. Fu's right hand gripped his left wrist atop Angus's left shoulder, torquing hard. He said, "When next you wake, you will be in the needles of purgatory." And Angus grunted, tried to struggle, but found the same darkness as Jarhead.

Purcell's bones creaked as he made it to his feet and asked, "What's your handle?"

Fu gripped Angus by his hair, pulled him off Jarhead, unbuckled Angus's belt, pulled it, bloody and stinking, from his waist. He rolled Angus facedown, tugged and laced his wrists tight behind him. Scanned his eyes over the money scattered across the barn floor. Turned to Purcell and asked, "Handle?"

Purcell said, "Your name."

"My name is Fu," he replied. "I have been hunting this man who calls himself Angus. He owes many debts."

Purcell pursed his lips, looked at the money on the floor, said, "Well, they's plenty for the taking. Me and Jarhead ain't a greedy bunch no ways, 'specially since you saved our asses."

Fu bowed to Purcell. He collected twenty grand in fifties and hundreds and neatly piled the money into a sack. There was plenty left over—he'd barely made a dent. Fu rolled Angus over his shoulder. Then stood, turned, and started to walk out the way he'd entered.

Purcell said, "I think we might be seeing you again. Just don't ask me what for."

Fu said, "Very well." Then disappeared.

The barn walls vibrated from the crowd's pounding. Purcell kneeled down. His back popped as he lifted Jarhead from the floor. His wound pulsed with ache as he stood up, balanced Jarhead, and led him out to the Bronco. He laid him across the backseat.

The man mumbled cherry-sized bubbles from his lips, and Purcell said, "Save it. We's two lucky sons a bitches. I gotta get some of McGill's loot sacked up 'fore them people out yonder figure out they's a rear end to this barn. They's fixing to hobble or lynch the each of us. We gotta make some dust."

PART IV
THE
BEGINNING

22

Angus's veins were burning with thorns. Sharp points dented the meridians of his body, taking away the strength to flex his limbs. Now he was a flaccid piece of chilled meat.

Opening his eyes, all he could see was dark. Inhaling, he smelt his own flesh, sweat, and soap.

He had turbulent flashes in his mind: water so cold his body felt more bare bone than flesh; bristles scrubbing the blood from him, ignoring the welts and bruises; a careful hand guiding a needle, pulling and meshing open wounds back together. Being placed into a glittering tomb molded to his form.

Angus tried to wiggle a finger or a toe but could not. He heard voices.

Outside the silver tomb, Fu stood in his basement attired in new glasses, black dress slacks, and a bright white T-shirt, scab-faced, with plum-tinted circles patching his complexion and arms. Three men stood in front of him. One Chinese. One black. One white. They wore black T-shirts tucked into black military slacks, shiny black combat boots. Each man had tattoos of his chosen discipline inked on his inner forearm. The Asian man showed a black tiger with gray stripes, the black man had a golden dragon engulfed by orange flames, and the white man had a golden snake surrounded by red flutes of bamboo. The man with the black tiger tattoo asked, "What'd you do with the cop?"

Fu smiled. "I used a needle to remove his memory. Then I dropped him in front of the hospital."

"And Mr. Zhong?"

"He is happy. His debt has been collected."

"What about the redneck named Pete?"

"He will adjust. Every student has a learning curve."

Black Tiger motioned toward the steel tomb, asked, "What happens if this man survives Si-Bok Lao's training, wants to come back here some day, maybe find you, maybe find the cop?"

"Let him. I trained each of you just as Lao trained me and the ones that will train him. I am the one who offers a second chance. He is unique, just as I was. It would be a waste to not let him use what he knows best."

Black Tiger said, "Fighting."

Fu nodded his head. "Yes, *fighting.*"

Black Tiger observed, "*Sifu.* He must be one very dangerous individual, the way you treated him. I've never seen you use so many needles."

Fu smiled. "One for every pressure point. He is helpless now. But without them, he is indeed dangerous. Menacing. He could one day be our equal."

The three men bowed to their *sifu,* their teacher. Fu stepped back, watched each man grab a side of the man-sized case and lift it.

Inside the steel tomb, Angus felt his body fall backward, listened to footsteps bounce from the concrete floor, echo off the walls. He searched for something inside of himself to squeeze—be it be an organ, tendon, or muscle—but he could not find anything he could control. All he could do was wonder where these men were taking him.

Outside, the three men loaded Angus into the rear of a black Tahoe. Fu observed with his hands behind his back. When the rear hatch was closed, the three students turned to Fu and he said, "This Angus knows how to use pain for nourishment. The more he is conditioned, the stronger he will become. He will not be an easy man to break."

Black Tiger asked, "We will see you soon?"

Fu said, "If he is alive in three months, yes. I look forward to it."

The three men bowed to Fu. Got into their Tahoe, started the engine, and headed down the paved drive.

23

Their Chevys and Fords lined the blacktop lot, some parked along old 64, loaded with clothing, grills, and their remaining choices of booze or drugs, their bodies snaked into the brick structure of Swaren's Funeral Home, each man and woman wanting a glimpse of the fallen, the person who'd been their center for so long, Bellmont McGill. Some tossing in things that held meaning to them—a pint of Beam, Turkey, or Old Granddad. Others gave double- and single-blade pocketknives passed down from long-gone kinfolk, or brass that had not been fired.

After the ceremony, the single file of cars that followed the hearse to the burial went for miles, all the way to where the Donnybrook had been held. Pallbearers came in worn denim, button-ups tucked, a few wore ties, some had hands bandaged and taped, eyes swollen, hair greased to the side or over the tops of heads. They stood in two formations, unloaded the dead, and trudged to the hole where McGill was to be lowered.

The blessing had been given and final respects were passed, the dirt shoveled down into the hole, over the coffin. Men, women, and fighters huddled in front of their beat, rusted, and scratched vehicles. And like the smoke that hung over the field from the barns that had been torched to chunks of rubble, an uncertainty remained on every patron's mind: Would there ever be another Donnybrook?

A few dogs ran about the grounds that were littered with paper, cans, bottles, chicken, and fish bones. Snarling and growling for a final taste of what had been.

Bellmont's stable of men stood like protectors brailled by ink, guns tucked into the hems of their waists. Knuckles nicked; eyes, noses, and lips botched and rent; their wounds flaking. All of them angered by the outcome but waiting for words of what would come next from Scar Mc-Gill. Thought to be dead, she was not, had only been pierced and riffled by bullets. She stood at the center of the unruly followers kneeling over the mound of dirt, knowing her father would be reunited with her mother, who'd been taken out by the booze that ruined her liver, then her life. But Scar, with her dirty-blond hair and oatmeal roots wavering in the breeze, a body full of ache and papered with bandage and bruise, she would pick up the pieces, bring a new generation of ideas and hell to the land and any person who lied about or hid the men she'd hunt, raising havoc along the highways and back roads until she found the ones who'd taken her father from her and the outlet he'd built for these people.

•

Tammy's green eyes glossed with worry watching the lights grow, detailing the trees and power lines that ran alongside the road.

One child suctioned his legs around Tammy's bony waist. The other was at her side, his tiny hand in her sweaty fist. Each child had chocolate milk hulling his lips, his hair parted in all directions.

Late evening air knuckled their skin. Crickets and katydids chirped in the wilderness that surrounded them like the approaching darkness. Two plastic grocery sacks lay at their feet with the necessities: pants, shirts, bra, panties, and a few diapers. The sound of tires crunching gravel grew in pitch.

Earlier, a phone's ringing had echoed throughout a rundown trailer. Tammy answered, "Hello?"

Jarhead said, "Be down at Blister Fork in four hours. Pack light."

Hearing the wear and tear in his tone, she asked, "You okay?"

Jarhead hesitated and said, "Been better."

She said, "It's been three damn days, did you . . . did you . . . win?"

He said, "They was no winner. Get packing." And hung up.

Now the rusted-out Bronco squeaked to a stop. Rocky dust fogged in front of the headlights. The engine rumbled. The Bronco's passenger-side door opened. Jarhead stepped out onto the road. His scooped-out muscled arms embraced Tammy and his boys, helped them into the back of the Bronco with the two sacks of their belongings. Zeek sat on Jarhead's lap, Caleb sat to his right. Tammy to his left.

The darkness inside the Bronco couldn't hide Tammy's melancholy any more than the shadows could hide the jagged purples fusing with the violets of Jarhead's lumped facade. Tammy held tight to Jarhead, nodded to the Bronco's driver, and asked, "Who is he?"

From the driver's seat, a set of worn eyes, one outlined in swelling from Angus's fist, caught Tammy's gaze in the rearview, and a voice said, "Name's Purcell."

Purcell shifted into drive, and Tammy said, "Mine's Tammy. Nice to make your acquaintance."

Purcell said, "Pleased to finally make yours, Tammy."

From the radio, Johnny Cash spoke with the crackle of static behind his voice: *And I heard as it were the noise of thunder, one of the four beasts sang come and see, and I saw and behold a white horse.*

Tammy pushed her head into Jarhead's chest and asked, "Where we going?"

Jarhead said, "To Dote's gun shop."

Tammy raised her head, looked at Jarhead, asked, "Dote's gunshop?"

Jarhead looked Tammy in the face and said, "I gotta pay back what I stole. And Purcell here wants to do a little shopping."

"For guns?"

Purcell looked in the rearview to Tammy and said, "We cashed out from the 'Brook by our hides. We got a sackful of cash, but we didn't make no friends there. There's some shit about to go down, and it's startin' right here in these counties. We need to make sure we're protected."

Confused, Tammy asked, "What kinda tongue is you talking?"

Jarhead gently grabbed her arm and silently nodded, his eyes expressing that he'd learned to trust this man, and so should she.

In the background Johnny Cash scratched at the strings of his acoustic guitar and began singing, *There's a man going around taking names, and he decides who to free and who to blame. Everybody won't be treated all the same, there'll be a golden ladder reaching down when the man comes around.*

Purcell rounded the curve, and a Shell gas station sat on the left. Jarhead eyed Purcell in the rearview and said, "Through the light, past Wendy's, and stop in front of the building next to it."

Purcell nodded.

Jarhead explained to Tammy, "Purcell sees things before they happen."

Tammy turned to Jarhead and asked, "He a fortune-teller?"

"Fortuneteller, soothsayer. He's seen change coming, violent change."

Tammy protested. "What's that got to do with us? Ain't you done enough?"

From the driver's seat Purcell said, "This is Jarhead's calling. Boy fights like an angel. We need him, we all need him."

Jarhead felt Tammy tremor with worry, pulled her close to his side with his left arm, his boys with his right, and said, "I believe what Purcell is saying." He turned and pressed his lips to Tammy's forehead and told her, "It'll be okay, Tammy, it'll be okay."

Purcell stopped in front of the gun shop. Reached across the passenger's seat to open the door.

Jarhead released Tammy, pushed the seat forward, sat Zeek next to Caleb, and stepped from the Bronco. Purcell

239

opened the driver's side and got out with a stack of crumpled bills. Looked across the Bronco's hood at Jarhead as they walked toward the gun shop and said, "Johnny, anything happens to me, remember this name: Van Dorn. No idea what it means. And another thing—you need to tell her that *it* ain't even started yet."

ACKNOWLEDGMENTS

Thanks to the early readers of the *Donnybrook* manuscript, Donald Ray Pollock, Anthony Neil Smith, Christa Faust, John Rector, Craig Clevenger, Victor Gischler, Kyle Minor, Jed Ayers, Scott Phillips, Keith Rawson, Roger Smith, Elaine Ash, David Cranmer, Israel Byrd, Denny Faith, and Ella Baker. You guys and gals kick ass.

To Scott Montgomery, for spreading the word and having me at the Book People. For the music of Ray Wylie Hubbard and for being a damn good friend and letting me know that if one were to cut my words with a knife, they'd bleed.

To Rod Wiethop, for being an early fan and a damn good friend.

To all of my martial arts and boxing teachers, John King, Tony Wood, Matt Kitterman, Eric Haycraft, Frank Sexton, and John Winglock Ng. Without your passing me your knowledge, wisdom, and discipline, I'd have never made it this far as a writer.

Thanks to my agent, Stacia J. N. Decker, for getting this into shape and not letting me take the easy way out, and to my kick-ass editors Sean McDonald and Emily Bell, for sound advice throughout the editing process.

Thanks to everyone at FSG, my copy editors, proofreaders, Rodrigo and the art/design people, and the foreign-rights department. And my publicist, Brian Gittis.

Most of all, thanks to my family and friends for coming to my readings and spreading the good word. Your support means the world to me. And to my mother and father for raising me on Clint Eastwood movies.